Somewhere in Minnesota

Kirk House Publishers

Somewhere in Minnesota

Short Stories

Jayna Locke

Paperback ISBN: 978-1-959681-50-2
eBook ISBN: 978-1-959681-51-9
Hardcover ISBN: 978-1-959681-52-6
Library of Congress Number: 2024904325

Photo Credit Cover: Jayna Locke
Photo Credit Author Headshot: Mary Jo Brokaw
Cover and Interior Design by Ann Aubitz
Published by Kirk House Publishers

Kirk House Publishers
1250 E 115th Street
Burnsville, MN 55337
612-781-2815
kirkhousepublishers.com

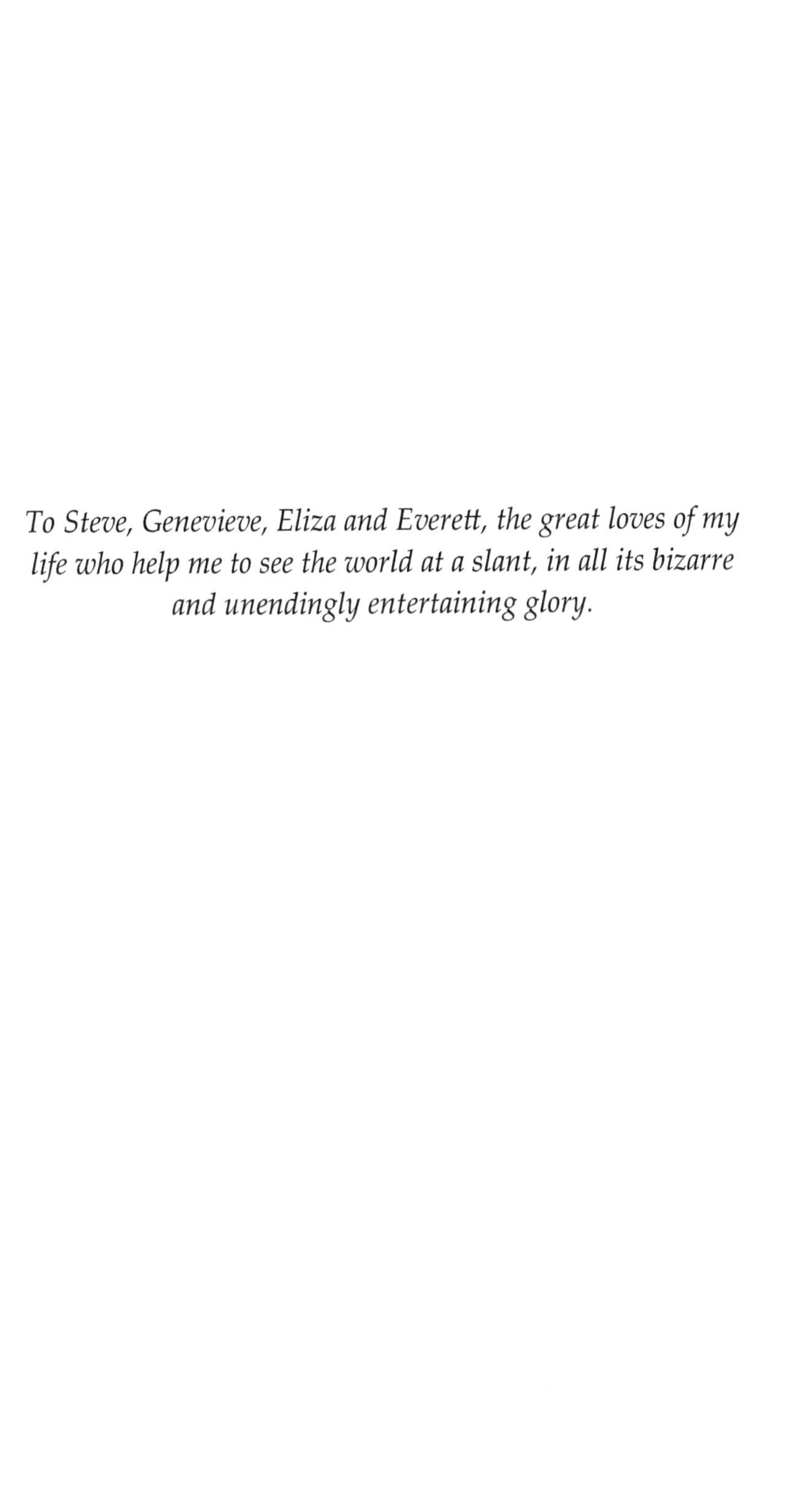

To Steve, Genevieve, Eliza and Everett, the great loves of my life who help me to see the world at a slant, in all its bizarre and unendingly entertaining glory.

Contents

1

Last Night in Fargo

The train pulls into St. Paul Union Station. My fellow passengers disembark and hustle off to wherever they are going. The last passenger off the train is a woman in a brown coat who detrains awkwardly with an oversized case and takes a desultory, gallows walk through the depot. I ponder what her story might be, as I scan the dissipating crowd for Carl. But he is not there. The train moves on down the tracks, picking up momentum as it chugs toward Chicago.

My phone buzzes—a text from Carl saying he's running late. "Big snarl on 94. There's a game at Vikings Stadium and something happening at the Armory."

"Please don't text and drive, Carl."

"It's hands-free, baby. The miracle of Siri."

We have always been like this. I tell him to use caution and he tells me that's nonsense. Our relationship is oblique in some ways, built on negotiations and patience. We don't talk about settling down, as we haven't figured out how to meet in the middle.

I walk through the station, restless, wondering if I'm homesick or just tired of traveling. Outside, listless snow flurries drift down from a marshmallow sky.

At last, Carl pulls up at the curb in our green Fiesta. He pops the trunk from inside. I lift my luggage in and slam down the hatch, irritation creeping over me like slime. I try to shake it off. I've been away for a week. Doesn't distance make the heart grow fonder?

"It's always busy on 94," I say, sliding into the passenger seat. "So you give yourself extra time."

"You're right, Teri. I'm sorry. How was Fargo?"

"It was fine. The client is happy. They placed a big order, so my boss is over the moon."

My mouth says these words, but my mind thinks about how Fargo was a complete escape. A world away.

And there was a man.

Each night I went to the same restaurant for a quiet dinner and a glass of wine. And each night he was there too—also on business from the Twin Cities. Eventually, we sat together, talked, had a second glass of wine. Then another. He spoke of his unhappy marriage.

"That's great, babe," Carl says. "I did the grocery shopping."

My mind travels back to the old game of telephone that my sisters and I played as children. The sounds came through, but the sensibility was lost. Cushion became pushing. Lamp became damp. And so sensible descriptions of everyday household items devolved into a string of ridiculous non sequiturs.

The freeway is lined with tired snow, shoved aside by plows and sullied by vehicle exhaust and road grit. This is the worst thing about Minnesota winters—the ugly aftermath of the storms.

Carl glances at me sideways. "Penny for your thoughts?"

I laugh without mirth as we pass the basilica with its grand, imposing dome. "That's about what they're worth right now. One rusted red cent. I'm so tired."

And yet what I'm really thinking about is the warmth of Samuel's hands. How we talked each night until the restaurant staff took away our silverware, napkins and glasses, and we finally paid up and parted ways.

"Hey," Carl says. "I have a surprise for you at home."

"Oh?"

My emotions tumble. I know what he's doing—trying to stitch us together again—because whenever we're apart, the strands that connect us twist and fray. He knows that a surprise is my one weakness. But is this what I want? To meld back into life with Carl? I don't know. I can't think. Can't speak.

Run from this, says my silent thought. *Run away.*

Last night in Fargo, at our final dinner together, I studied Samuel's face glowing by candlelight. What I saw there was pure yearning. For *me*. My heart shivered, not knowing how to say goodbye.

My phone buzzes and I glance down. It is *him*. "Can I see you?"

Maybe? Maybe. I silence my phone without responding. The feel of Samuel's touch is fading away like the shadows of a dream.

At home, the driveway is cleared of snow, the sidewalk swept. I wheel my luggage toward the house, remembering the gallows walk of the woman at the depot. And then I am inside, shaking off the chill. I smell scented candles burning. Lavender and patchouli. The gas fire is lit. Fresh flowers burst from a vase on the island counter.

"Now for the surprise," Carl says. "Close your eyes."

He leads me through the house. A blind woman, out of place, unable to find her way.

He opens a door, and I know where we are. It is the spare room, where we store the unkempt matter of our lives—old boxes of photographs, discarded DIY projects.

"Okay, open your eyes!"

Two kittens sit in a fleecy bed looking up with pale eyes. They are tiny wobbly things. They stretch and yawn.

Correction, I think. I have two weaknesses.

I pick them up and they smell of sweetness and sleep and the need for love.

"Oh Carl. They are precious. What are their names?"

He shrugs. "We can pick them."

Then he turns to face me, and his eyes are glistening. *He knows. Oh god, he knows.*

He presses his lips together. Blinks. Then he says, "Choose me. Please. I mean, of course it's up to you. But honey, please… choose me."

I nod. The clam shell of my heart cracks open. The kittens purr in my arms, and I hold them close. I am home.

Author's note: Last Night in Fargo was first published in July, 2023 in The Talking Stick Volume 32 anthology: A Twist in the Road, by The Jackpine Writers Bloc.

2

Prodigal Father

The man at the door was graying and tattered looking, like old laundry that won't come clean. A bum, was my first guess. Someone looking for a hand-out.

Mom shooed the girls and the dog away and pulled me back from the door with an impatient tug. When she opened it, the bum walked right in. And there we were all standing in a nervous cluster—Mom, the disheveled man, the three of us kids and our growling beagle, Mary Jane, a renowned ankle biter.

Then I figured it out and snapped my fingers. *Dad.*

Mom had Mary Jane by the collar. "Go outside and play, kids," she said. "And take the dog. Now."

The three of us and Mary Jane marched out to the backyard, even though there was a cold Minnesota breeze blowing. It was November. The leaves had fallen weeks ago, and we crunched through them, trying to find our Frisbees and balls, some of which wouldn't turn up until the snowmelt in the spring.

I didn't think much about my dad being in the house. I was 12 and had better things to do. He'd high-tailed it out of our lives when I was five, restless and angry, and hadn't so much as sent a holiday card since.

"Let's build a fire," I said. This seemed the most logical thing to do.

Penny looked at me like I was testing her last nerve. Typical. "No, Max. That is not happening." She was 15, and the boss of us three when Mom wasn't around.

But Jillian, who was seven, had come out without a sweater. She looked at Penny and sniffed like she was coming down with something. "But I'm cold."

I pulled a matchbox from my pocket and held it up for the girls to see, proud that I had come prepared. "A fire it is!"

Penny snatched the matchbox out of my hand. "Give me those. Are you out of your mind?"

"No. I'm a Fire Safety Merit-Badge-wearing Boy Scout." I tried to grab the matches back. "Hey. C'mon. They're mine."

I had earned the merit badge by doing a full fire hazard check of the house and visiting a fire station. I even made us all crawl on the floor to safety, while holding cloths over our mouths to block imaginary smoke. Also, I had demonstrated safe use of matches.

To show Penny that I knew what I was doing, I gathered leaves, and some newspapers that were stacked in the shed, and began assembling it all in the fire pit, with twigs arranged in a teepee formation.

Jillian was hopping around trying to stay warm, her breath coming out in white puffs, as if we had all stepped into a big cryogenic chamber. "Hey," she said. "Who's that man?"

Penny and I looked at each other, and I waved my hand toward the unlit fire in the manner of a magician. "Go ahead," I said. "Do the honors."

She took out a match and slid it along the rough brown strip of the matchbox. Nothing happened. She glanced at Jillian and said, "He's your father." She tried the match again with the same result.

Jillian had never known our dad at all, because she was an infant when he left us, and he had never once been back. Until now. She shook her head as if the idea that the man in the house could be a close relation was rattling around in there like a bug in a jar.

Penny handed me the matchbox.

"You have to press down," I said. I demonstrated the technique. "But you keep your fingers away, like this." A small flame came to life, and I lit the papers and kindling and pretty soon Jillian and Penny gathered close to stay warm. I added some larger kindling and then a couple of logs from the woodpile by the shed and soon the fire was crackling hot.

This mission accomplished, I looked for something else to do. I slugged Jillian on the arm, but she didn't slug back. "Come on, let's play catch." Both of my sisters stared at me like Mary Jane does when she knows you want to give her a bath.

It was times like these when I wished for a brother. I remembered thinking all the while I was little that a kid should have someone to punch. Someone to roughhouse with. I imagined wrestling on the floor, shooting cans in the backyard with BB guns, and throwing lassos with rope. Mary Jane would have been the perfect little wild horse to practice on. By the time I met my friend Greg we were both 10 going on 11, and I was mostly past thinking those things were interesting. Still, Greg and I liked boxing. And video games. And girls.

It was evident that my sisters were just going to stand there by the fire, but I wanted to chuck a ball around or do something fun. Mary Jane was in a pile of leaves chewing on a stick. So I climbed the tree and looked down on my sisters like the Cheshire Cat.

"Lose something?" I quoted.

Penny looked up. "Get down from there before you fall."

She had that stark, worried look around the eyes that happened whenever she was stressed out, like when she had a big test at school, or wanted some boy to ask her to a dance. At those times I could see what she would look like when she was much older, and life had given her a few hard tumbles.

Jillian stared at the house. "What's he doing here?"

I called down, "He's come to take you away, ha ha!"

"Max!" Penny put her arm around Jillian. "Don't listen to that brat."

Jillian stuck her tongue out at me.

Then our parents walked out of the house, and the screen door made its characteristic slam, just as if it was summertime and the aroma of the tomato vines in the sun was wafting out of the garden.

Our dad took his hands out of his overall pockets and crossed them over his chest as he surveyed us. Then he looked at Mom. "You just let them make a fire?"

Mom looked at him with a kind of whiplash move, which suggested to me that things weren't going so well. What would you expect after seven years? I wondered what they had talked about in the house. Then I spied something near me in the tree. Just on the edge of my peripheral vision, there was a tinge of blue. An abandoned robin's nest with three tiny perfect blue eggs, cold but preserved, lay before my very eyes. It was a wonder that they hadn't been eaten by raccoons.

Down below, Penny still had her arm wrapped around Jillian's shoulder. Jillian asked, "Are you my dad?"

"Yes. Hello… sweetheart." He didn't seem to know what to call us.

I pried up the bird's nest, very carefully, to make sure the eggs wouldn't go flying. As tempting as it was to drop one onto each of the girls' heads, I thought better of it. I wanted to show them to Greg, who was visiting his dad in Michigan for Thanksgiving.

The stand-off in the yard continued. Our dad had taken a step toward the girls, the way you might sneak up on wildlife. And Penny had taken a step back toward the fire. I suppose she remembered him the best. She was eight when he left, half her lifetime ago. Maybe she was sad that he went away, or maybe upset he'd come back. You never know with girls.

I had wrapped the nest up in my flannel shirt when I looked down and saw Mom at the base of the tree, looking up at me.

"Come down, Max. You're not being a very good host right now."

So, there were rules to follow when your father returns home after being away for-freaking-ever. Or maybe these were the same rules that would apply if you were visited by an old friend or a distant relative. Someone you knew only from a vague memory or a fading picture in a photo album.

"Alrighty."

I was only wearing my t-shirt now, having removed the flannel layer to make a kind of sling for the nest, and my arms were covered in goose bumps. If I'd had a stick, I could have made an old-timey bindle I had seen in pictures of hobos walking down long dusty roads or along railroad tracks. One time Greg had even dressed up like one for Halloween and we made him a bindle out of a red kerchief tied around some socks.

I straddled a thick branch with my legs and leaned down out of the tree holding out the carefully wrapped parcel. "Would you take this, Mom?"

She accepted it the way a person might receive a bouquet, arms outstretched, unsure of how to get a purchase on something so delicate yet awkward.

"Don't tip it. Please keep it level." I let go and jumped down, landing with a pretty cool ninja move, if I do say so myself.

Mom handed me the makeshift bindle. "Come on, we're all going inside. We're going to chat."

"A family meeting," our dad said.

For that he got another look from Mom, who had taken Jillian's hand and was walking past him.

In the living room, we sat in various chairs. Mom had appropriated the big armchair. Jillian had climbed onto her lap, and was snuggled in. I half expected Jilly to stick her thumb in her mouth, a habit she had finally given up about a year and a half before. Once a baby, always a baby.

But Penny looked lost. The options were admittedly not great. Our dad was sitting in one of the two velveteen padded chairs across from Mom and Jillian. So there was only one more of those, right next to him. Or there was the couch, which always made a farting sound if you sat on it. No kidding. It sounded exactly like a fart. Greg and I loved it, but no one ever sat on the couch when we had other guests. In fact, if anyone came over, we would sort of body-check them away from the fart couch, and then gesture meaningfully toward one of the velveteen chairs so they wouldn't even consider it.

I grabbed the good cushion from the couch, chucked it on the floor and sat on that, and Mary Jane settled next to me, having satisfied herself that the man in our house was not an immediate threat. Penny sat on the arm of the couch, her back straight. It looked about as comfortable as sitting on a barbed wire fence. I couldn't read her expression. It was as if she had none at all.

Mom adjusted a bit because Jillian was all sharp bones and if she ever sat on you, you were likely to get poked by one of them.

"Now then," Mom said.

Then she went quiet. She looked around at all of us, and there was a long pause. What do you say when your family loses an appendage and then it tries to reattach itself?

I suddenly thought of Frankenstein and felt a laugh coming on. I had to pinch myself on the tender part of my arm, just above the elbow, to make it stop. But then I thought of the word "wenis," which Greg had informed me was the technical term for elbow skin and I couldn't contain myself. A sort of burp laugh splurted out of me, and everyone looked at me like I was from Mars. So I put my face in my hands for a moment, hoping it would look like I was overcome with emotion.

Mom filled the silence. "This is your father. Your *dad*."

Next, I wondered if she would try out words for male parental figures in other languages.

"And," she continued. "He would like to spend time with us."

I wanted to pretend we were in court and shout "Objection, your honor!" It would have been funny. Mary Jane looked up at me because I was shaking a little, trying not to laugh.

"Yes."

This came from our dad who looked to me like an old man, now, sitting in the graying haze of the late afternoon—the air smudged by smoke from our dying backyard fire. Plus, it seemed no one had thought to turn on a light. And in that muted space, he appeared to be aging by the minute and shrinking into the chair.

We all waited for him to say something more. But he just nodded, as if "yes" was the sum total of his wisdom on the matter.

Mom sighed. "So, I've invited him for Thanksgiving. And of course your cousins will be here. It's going to be quite the party."

Penny looked stunned.

"Now," Mom continued. "What do you kids have to say?"

I searched my mental rule book. Somewhere there must be the statute about what you're supposed to say when your mom invites a stranger who is also your dad to a special holiday. I came up with nothing.

She looked at each of us in turn, starting with Penny.

"No comprendo," Penny said. She was studying Spanish, and evidently this was her out.

Mom gave her a mildly stern look and seemed to be struggling with how hard to force the issue. But it wasn't really in her nature to be strict. Mom was the kind of person who would threaten a beating or say she was going to withhold allowance but was too soft inside to carry it out. "Penny…."

But before Mom could finish her sentence, Penny got up and walked out. Then Jilly climbed off of Mom's lap and ran after her.

I shrugged. "Sure as shootin'. We have a damn fine Thanksgiving around here, old man."

I don't know what possessed me to talk like I just stepped off the set of an old western, but I felt kind of good about it. Like I could be someone completely new, if I wanted. My dad didn't even know me, so what did it matter? I could be a jock, a greaser, a druggy, or a country line dancer, if I chose. Whatever I said, he'd just have to believe.

Mom was giving me the look. It's that one that all moms give their children when they want them to stop being kids—when for at least a little while they would like to see them acting like adults.

In the chair across the room, the man who would be joining us for Thanksgiving dinner, who wanted to try on being our dad again, rose slowly like Jack's beanstalk until he towered over both of us, and I had to wonder which he was—the shrunken aging man, or the giant.

"I'll be on my way," he said. "May I bring anything tomorrow? A pie? A bottle of wine?"

Mom stood from her chair to look him in the eye with an unwavering stare, and I realized something in that moment about strength and power.

"Anything you like," she said. "We serve at six o'clock." Then she moved toward the front door, where Dad was expected to follow.

Later as I was watching stuff on Netflix, Greg texted me to ask how it was going.

"Dude. How's it going?"

"Whatup. Big feast tomorrow." I didn't know what else to say. "Plus, there's a ghost here. Ha ha."

He sent a raised eyebrow emoji. Then I saw the little dots that indicated he was typing something. "My dad's a vegetarian. So we're having something else. Toofuckie I think."

I typed a laughing emoji. "That sucks man."

"Tell me about it. Save some meat for me."

"No probs."

As I began to fall asleep, I thought about how Greg was the brother I never had.

♦　♦　♦

Our relatives came at three o'clock in the afternoon — Aunt Renee and Uncle Zeke, and our cousins Lisa, Portia and Teddy. Mary Jane practically exploded from excitement and so we had to get her all settled. Of course I acted completely chill and composed, but actually I was excited too, because then we had kids to hang out with. Mom had help from her sister and brother-in-law, which let us off the hook after an afternoon of KP duty and dusting.

Penny and Jillian ran off to do girl things with Lisa and Portia. Teddy wanted to see my room. He was only six and he pretty much idolized me. Tough gig for me, but I accepted my plight.

"What's this? And this?" Teddy went around my room pointing at things and asking about all of my crap. It was just stuff, but maybe to a little kid it seemed exotic.

I showed him my butterfly collection, which included a perfect monarch I had found dead in a field and a Polyphemus moth. Greg had personally caught it for me, and even though it was just a moth, it was my favorite.

Teddy stared at it for a moment then looked up at me. "Can it see me?" He was mesmerized by the wings, which had two large black marks that looked like eyes.

"No silly. Those are the moth's markings. They scare off attackers."

Then I showed him all my merit badges, and my tracking book where I logged all the stuff I had to do for the badges I was working on. Also, I taught him how to make three types of knots, which was kind of tough for his little hands.

"You'll do better when you're older," I said.

I thought we should go downstairs soon, but he was enjoying my box of feathers and shells, including my most prized possession—the shell of a small turtle. I didn't have the heart to pull him away.

"Oh, look at this," I said. I reached up on the shelf in my closet where I had put the nest the day before. I brought it down but held it up high over his head for a moment. "This is the newest addition to my collection. But when I show it to you, you've got to promise not to touch."

He nodded, and when I lowered the nest to just below his eye level so he could see the three sky-blue eggs, his eyes went wide. "Whoa, are they real?"

"Of course, dummy."

"But I mean, will they hatch?"

I laughed. "No, the nest was abandoned. So these won't hatch. They're just pretty to look at." Right then, I thought of Penny, Jillian and me.

"You're so lucky, Max."

"What?

"You get to keep things." He began clomping around the room in the heavy boots I bought at the army surplus store. He was also carrying my BB gun over his shoulder. I silently begged for no one to show up at my door just then. He stopped marching to look at me. "What's it like to have a mom who lets you collect stuff?"

I shrugged. "Hell, I don't know. What's it like to have a dad?"

Teddy's head tilted exactly the way a dog does when it doesn't quite get your meaning. Maybe he hadn't realized before that there was never a dad at our house. Only a mom and three kids. But he didn't have an answer. He just looked a little sorry. You don't think about not having something until you see yourself through the eyes of someone who does.

"C'mon," I said. "I'll show you how to slide down the banister."

Downstairs everyone was milling about the kitchen and the dining room. It smelled perfect. Like every Thanksgiving I could ever remember. Mom and Renee kept leaning close to talk quietly, and at one point I heard mom say, "He's not a bad man. He's just… you know… broken."

Maybe she thought no one could hear because it was so noisy in the kitchen. But my superpower is that I can focus my hearing on whatever I want and tune out everything else. Plus I can read lips. I knew she had to be talking about my dad. And that's when I realized he hadn't arrived yet. It was almost six o'clock.

Uncle Zeke called all the kids into the living room to show us magic tricks. He was amazing and I decided I needed to take it up as a hobby. I kept trying to see how he was doing it, and I was completely into it, even though I knew the whole reason for this little magic trick session was a distraction because we were hungry, but we had to wait. He showed us nothing was up his sleeve, but then a moment later pulled a card out. He found a coin behind Penny's ear. We all kept asking for one more.

Trying not to sound too hopeful, I said, "Will you show me how?"

He gave me a grin. "Of course. After dinner, okay?"

Finally, at twenty minutes after six, the doorbell rang. Uncle Zeke excused himself to answer the door and Mary Jane ran along behind him, then growled again when the door opened, and it turned out to be my prodigal father.

"Hey old Zzzeke." The emphasis on the Z was troubling.

Uncle Zeke widened the door. "Come in, Jay."

"Well I should shthink so. It's my house."

Penny looked at me, blinking. She must have had every kind of emotion going on. "He's impaired," she said to me.

I was pretty sure that was the same as drunk.

Jillian stood behind Penny, looking out at our dad. I wanted to tell her that Penny was probably not the best shield. She looked frail as a wilting flower.

Uncle Zeke clapped our dad on the back as if for reassurance, but then used his grip on Dad's shoulder to steer him toward the dining room. I noticed Dad was empty handed, so he had not brought a pie or anything as he said he would. I imagined him stopping at the nearby park on the way, and guzzling the bottle of wine he was supposed to bring, like it was medicine for a sickness.

Shortly we were all at the table and my mom said a prayer and we began to pass the bowls of potatoes and stuffing and cranberry sauce.

"I think we'll get some snow tomorrow," Renee said.

That was the funny thing about meals with guests. Polite conversation was required. If my dad hadn't been there, we would all have been chattering on about real stuff.

Mom smoothed the napkin in her lap. "Yes. It will be nicer for getting a Christmas tree, if there's snow."

In the pause that happened then, you could hear forks and knives on plates and the sound of chewing. Aunt Renee took a sip of her wine and looked around as if she wanted to say something but could think of nothing. So she just smiled at her husband and cut another bite of turkey.

I couldn't remember a Thanksgiving ever before when it wasn't noisy with people talking and laughing. I wanted to do something. Maybe it was the Boy Scout in me, wanting to be helpful. I said to my dad, "Uncle Zeke is going to teach me magic tricks."

A suspicious look crossed over Dad's face. "Izzat so?" He had just reached for the bowl of mashed potatoes, but now he just held it, as if he had forgotten what he intended to do.

"Yeah, he's really good at it," I said. "A total ace."

Penny had been poking at her food, but now she looked at me, frowning, and I felt her kick me under the table. There were more rules, apparently. Maybe you weren't supposed to talk about magic at Thanksgiving. Or maybe you couldn't compliment one man if there were two in the house.

Teddy drank from his glass of milk, then set it down and looked at my dad. "Who are you?"

"Now Teddy," Renee said.

At the same time, Mom said, "Well he is…." but she didn't seem able to say who or what he was. And maybe we all wondered the same thing as Teddy. Who are you?

Finally, she said, "He is Penny's, Max's and Jillian's father."

I didn't care what she called him. What did it matter? But I saw Penny flinch.

Then Teddy spoke again, this time to me. "I thought you said you didn't have a dad."

The room went silent. Dad was still holding the bowl of mashed potatoes. After a moment, he said, "Oh, is that how it is? I don't exist, huh? You got Zeke, so what do you need me for?"

He looked around the room, accusing each of us with furious, bloodshot eyes, perhaps expecting us to answer, to confess that yes, when he left all those years ago, we figured things out. We kept on going.

And that's when he dropped the mashed potato bowl. It crashed like a bomb going off, shattering both the bowl and the plate. Everyone jumped out of their chairs, bumping the table, which caused wine glasses to fall and explode, sending wine and glass shrapnel flying. All of the kids screamed.

People started reaching for dinner napkins to mop things up. Portia was crying, and Renee ran to her to pull a needle of broken glass from her hand.

Dad stood, his hands up in the air as if at gunpoint by a sheriff. "Okay, okay! I'm going!"

He pushed his chair back violently, then he lurched toward the door, flung it open, and was running down the stairs into the wind before anyone could do anything about it. He had left his coat on the back of his chair. Zeke grabbed it, plus a set of car keys and went after him.

The dinner was ruined, sprinkled with bits of China and glass.

I began to help Mom clean up the mess, while Penny helped Renee with the other kids. Some of the kids were crying. Penny seemed to collect herself. I saw her bandage Portia's hand gently while saying sweet things, like a mother would.

As I swept the floor, I suddenly remembered my last Thanksgiving with my dad. It was as if it had been hidden away in some weird memory vault until that very moment.

The memory was from Thanksgiving when I was five. Everything was all set for the feast and Mom was putting things on the table. Penny, who wore a yellow dress, was helping her. And Jillian, an infant, sat in a baby swing. I had heard my parents arguing earlier. Angry words. But it wasn't the first time. I thought they would just get over it. Like always.

We were about to sit down. Something was said between my parents, then. I don't remember what. Or maybe I never heard it at all. It's lost somewhere in the dense shadows of time.

I do remember this. Suddenly, my dad grabbed my hand. "Come on, son. We're going out."

Of course I went with him. He was my dad. And soon we were driving along the dark streets of town, with hardly anyone else out on that quiet night. We had turkey dinner at the Perkins on Highway 7, and then slices of pumpkin pie with whipped cream on top. And I felt a little happy, but a little sad. I was having time with just my dad. But there was also another meal back home. At the time I didn't know it would be the last meal I would have with my father.

I don't know how I could have forgotten that it was Thanksgiving when we started the process of living without him. Maybe my brain didn't want to remember how it felt to have my family splintering off, or maybe I felt nothing. As if that was just how things went sometimes. And then you figured out a new plan the next day. For Dad, the plan was to move on. The next morning when we woke up, he was gone.

After that we waited for him to come back and jumped every time the doorbell rang or a package was delivered, and then eventually we stopped. We became a family of four. And we got Mary Jane.

"I'm still hungry," Jillian said, when everything had settled down.

Mom stroked her hair. "Poor baby."

Renee had her arms around her kids too, except for Teddy, who sat on my lap. "We're okay," she said. "We're all okay."

I looked at Penny. She was generally my source for determining whether such statements were true. And sure enough, she looked like a person whose team just won, with a small yet triumphant smile making her look even prettier than she normally did on Thanksgiving.

Fortunately, the turkey carcass was in the kitchen, away from the wreckage of broken things, and still had plenty of meat on it. The pies and a backup supply of mashed potatoes were safe too. So that's what we had for dinner. It didn't seem like a bad deal at all.

Eventually Uncle Zeke came back alone and had pie too. He didn't mention my dad, or where he'd gone. And the whole thing seemed to be over. At that moment, I didn't know I'd never see my dad again. I guess reality unfolds in its own good time. Eventually we learned he had simply moved on again, traveling some wandering route in search of happiness.

Two days later, Greg got back from the trip to his father's house in Michigan and we went to my room to get away from the girls. He had a purple-green bruise in the shape of a half-moon under his left eye that he wouldn't talk about, even though I kept bugging him. I asked if he was maybe in a gang fight, or helped stop a bank robbery, but it didn't seem to be anything like that.

"Let's just say my dad and I don't get along real well," he said finally. But then he shifted the subject. "How about you? Anything interesting happen?"

I shook my head. "Nah, not really. Except I found a cool robin's nest. It had three abandoned eggs in it. But they're perfect."

"No kidding," he said. "That doesn't seem possible."

Then I remembered. "Oh! Plus, I saved you some turkey and some pie."

"Bro, you are the best."

That was when we did our secret handshake, and everything went back to normal.

3

Ripples

When the toddler walked out onto the ice, the birds were singing. Spring had come to Minnesota. But as always in early spring, the lakes retained a layer of ice that was riddled with small, dark, silky pools, and it remained for a few weeks after the air warmed. This restless state between winter and spring invited various living things to navigate the lake's icy surface—ducks, geese, foxes—and one small toddler named Jeffy.

Jeffy's mother was raking up the fallen leaves that had come down in October, just before the first snowfall. They had remained in wait through the long cold winter, and the chilly early spring, while the snow that had covered the flat lawn and descending hillside by the lake gradually diminished until only small white hillocks remained. Jeffy's father was cleaning the boat in anticipation of the formal "ice out" announcement and eventually the fishing opener. Jeffy's mother and father both thought the other had him in sight. And he had never strayed far.

Jeffy had played with his red ball on the flat part of the lawn for a while, after resurrecting it from the stow-away bin of toys that spent the winter under the deck. While he had only just taken his first baby steps back in the fall as the Minnesota winter loomed, now he could run like the wind. It was wonderful to be out in the cool air. He threw the red ball in the air and squealed when it landed on his head. Then it bounced away. And when he ran to pick it up, his little boot accidentally kicked it. To his delight it flew across the grass. But it continued over the edge of the lawn and tumbled downhill, then bounced onto the icy lake.

Madeline looked up from her raking. She saw Mitch, handsome in his muscle shirt, working on the boat. She saw their dog, Hercules, chewing a bone he had rediscovered after the snow melt. She scanned the yard and did not see Jeffy.

"Hon? You got Jeffy, right?"

"No. You have him. Don't you?"

They turned their eyes to the lake, which just weeks before had been frozen solid and dotted with ice fishing houses. Now the melting had begun in earnest. The ice houses had all been hauled off. There was nothing on the lake. Nothing except one Canada goose standing in the sun as if willing the oncoming spring to come, and one toddler, chasing after a red ball.

There was a stunned moment in which Madeline dropped the rake and Mitch dropped his arms to his sides. Then they began to run. They were down the hill to the edge of the lake in just a few heartbeats. But there they stopped. The shallow edge of the lake glistened with water that was eager to find sunlight, eager to push back the massive sheet of melting ice. The two adults clasped hands, then let go again. They could be of no support to one another now. What were they to do? They stepped tentatively closer to the lake's edge, as if they were afraid their very movement could vibrate the ice and send a crack slithering across its surface.

Their little boy was trying to catch the ball. But it was so light, and the breeze teased at it, shoving it along a little further and a little further, just as Jeffy approached. He giggled. It was such a silly game.

"Jeffy, honey," Madeline called out. "It's Momma." She used the soothing voice she reserved for fevers and night terrors. "Please stay where you are."

It was not immediately apparent how Jeffy had gotten out there. There was a foot of dark water between the shoreline and the crust of ice. Madeline's eyes darted around. Then, just downhill and to the left, she noticed a small bridge of ice the width of a plank. Just enough to support a small boy.

Mitch grimaced. Then he nodded. "I'm going out."

"No, Mitch! You've got 40 pounds on me. I'll go."

But the fact was, and they both knew this, the lake ice was unlikely to support either of them, even if they did find a way to get out there.

Jeffy had picked up the ball, at last, about 30 feet out. He was walking back toward them. The ice made a creaking, brittle sound with each step. He slowed, as if those sounds now registered, and he suddenly knew that at any moment he could plunge through a fissure in the ice and disappear into its depths. He stopped. "Momma?"

She held up her hand. "Baby, just wait. Wait right there." She knew he was safer the further away from them he remained.

Mitch patted his pockets for his phone, and not finding it said, "I'm going up to the house. Just… keep an eye on him. I'll call 9-1-1. And I'll bring something. Rope. Or… I don't know."

"Okay."

Mitch turned and began sprinting uphill.

"Momma?" Jeffy took two steps forward.

"No baby." She shook her head. "Stay right there." Tears were sliding down her face, chilling her cheeks. The temperature was dropping. She wrapped her arms around herself. "Please," she said under her breath, not knowing what she was asking for. "Please please please."

Mitch was the one who took care of all the bad things that happened in their lives—stopped up toilets, giant spiders, the snapping turtle that had been hit by a car in front of their house and was not quite dead. She glanced up the hill. He had only been gone a minute, but it seemed like hours. And here was Jeffy, walking slowly toward her, occasionally putting his arms up the way he did when he was tired and wanted to be picked up. She could see now that nothing was going to stop him. She had to do something.

Then she saw it—the canoe they had brought out of storage just the day before and set out on the canoe rack, even though it would be weeks before they would have open water. But it had been a fresh day, and the desire to air things out and prepare for the oncoming spring had been overwhelming.

"The neighbors will think we're nuts," Mitch had said.

"Oh let them," she had replied. "We will be ready the moment we can put in." She had dreamed of the warm days to come, never thinking that the canoe would come in handy even with the lake still covered in a sheet of ice.

Quickly, she pulled the canoe down and slid it down the embankment and onto the ice. It shushed into the watery edge, landing partly in water and partly on ice, then settled there at a tilt. Carefully, she stepped down into the canoe, gripping its sides. The edge of the ice creaked and gave way, shattering beneath the craft. She gasped as a crack broadened beneath the canoe and began spreading outward in all directions. In the distance, she heard a siren.

Jeffy had stopped walking. Lake water was pooling on the surface of the ice between them.

Then Madeline yelled. "Run, Jeffy!" She reached toward him from the canoe, holding out her arms.

And he ran, water splashing under his boots. He slipped and went sprawling, cracking the ice further. He was crying.

Madeline called out to him. "Keep going, baby! You can do it!"

He pulled himself up. His little jumpsuit was wet, and his face was a purplish pink from the cold and from crying. He stepped forward, with cracks spreading all around. Finally, he ran the last six feet to her, and she lifted him into the canoe, cradling him in her arms as Mitch and two EMTs descended the hill to them, carrying ropes, a harness, a lifeboat and blankets.

Years later, when this story had become family lore—just a small piece of fabric in the quilt of their lives—they would see this event in very different ways.

In Madeline's version, Mitch's leaving the lake to go for help was the only reason she came up with a plan and saved Jeffy. She would have waited for Mitch to think of something, otherwise. Until that moment, she had no idea she could ever do something brave. She had felt braver, stronger, ever since.

Mitch was not fond of this narrative, as it suggested the only reason Jeffy was saved was because he—Mitch—left the very scene where his little boy was in ultimate danger.

"I had to go," he said. "It was the only way to contact emergency services. If he had slipped through, then what would we have done?"

But of course, he hadn't arrived in time. The boy had already been saved by then, robbing him of the satisfaction.

Madeline rolled her eyes. "Honey, you're missing my point."

"Seriously, you guys?" Jeff, who was 17, no longer went by "Jeffy." He could remember very little of the incident, except for the feeling of want. He had wanted to go get his ball, then he had wanted to come back. That was all. "I can't believe you're fighting about this again."

He was right, of course. Mitch and Madeline knew this. They smiled at him, conceding that arguing about it was senseless. And it was so long ago. Still. This one point, as small as it seemed, was like a fissure on the surface of the earth, under which is a deep canyon.

"You know what I think?"

Mitch and Madeline looked at Jeff with expectation.

"I went out to get the ball, and then I came back, re-tracing my steps. I was small. Light as a feather. I would have just returned the way I had gone. You might not ever have noticed I was missing."

"What?"

"You mean…"

He nodded. And just like that, the tides shifted. Jeff's parents reached for each other and held hands, united in the knowledge that without them he would have died out on the lake that day, swallowed by the cold dark waters.

Author's note: Ripples was first published in April 2020 in Portage Magazine.

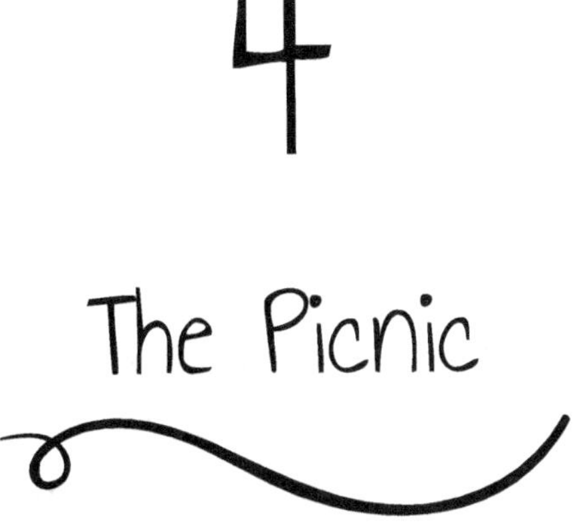

4

The Picnic

Megan circles a date on the calendar with a black permanent marker. When she turns to me, her hazel eyes shine in that mildly ferocious way of hers.

"Is that date okay, Josh?"

I look on with interest but don't quite know what to say, because it's only the tenth of January, and the proposed picnic is in late May. It feels like light years from now, in some distant galaxy.

And at that moment, it seems to me that there are two types of people in this world—those who mark calendars for points along the way to some future time, like Megan, and those who thrive in blissfully uncharted territory, like me. The Megans of the world love advent calendars and planners with little boxes where appointments are carefully noted down. I'm not criticizing. It's just that you can put something on the calendar and proclaim that in the future this will be this and that will be that… but then reality will rear its ugly head. The fact is, we don't have any idea what tomorrow will bring.

"Far as I know, that works for me," I tell her. "But… I mean, anything could come up in that time. Just saying."

"It's a date, then."

The look on her face is meaningful in a way I can't fathom. My inner self shrugs. It contemplates the reality of our relationship, which is by turns obfuscating and intoxicating.

We leave the apartment to go to a coffee shop, our Saturday morning routine. Megan's favorite one is the Caribou Coffee in the little town of Wren Lake because it's rarely too loud or busy, even on a frosty Minnesota morning like this one. We go in her car because she is not fond of the way I drive. She has told me various reasons why. "You don't hold your foot steady. It makes the car jerk. It's like riding with a squirrel."

I just nod when she tells me these things. Sometimes I imagine us years down the road, when I've given up trying to sort out our power dynamics and just say "yes dear." I invariably experience a small tornado in my head at the thought of it.

Our married friends, Neil and Rashmi, are at the coffee shop. They are holding hands, for some reason, while they drink coffee and eat scones.

Megan takes my hand to show we are a happy couple also. "Hey, hey! Look who's here," she says.

They stand up for hugs. First Rashmi hugs Megan, then Neil hugs her. Then Rashmi hugs me and Neil claps me on the shoulder. I have a brief feeling of Deja vu, but I think maybe it's because this greeting feels staged, not because it is one that has happened before.

Then it's time for decisions to be made. We could join them by scooching up a couple of chairs. Unless, of course, they want to be alone. In which case, we could go to another table. And if that is how it's going to roll, we could choose one nearby or further away. The choices are daunting. No one wants to be the one to say.

Megan looks expectantly at Neil and Rashmi and I feel a tinge of heat around my ears. It happens when I'm uncomfortable. I can see that she wants to be invited to sit together with them, and they don't understand why we are still standing there. The awkwardness is silly because we love these guys. We often hang out with them on Saturday nights and play Settlers of Catan and drink craft beer. But this is different. It's out of context.

Finally, Rashmi pipes up. "Please, join us!" So, we pull up chairs.

And that's when it becomes clear that Rashmi and Neil are in the middle of an argument. I kick myself for not seeing it. Rashmi's eyes are glassy, and Neil has that drawn look of a man who has dug himself a hole and doesn't know how to get back out. I want to signal to Megan somehow. But it's too late for that.

She pats Rashmi's arm a little aggressively. "We haven't seen you guys in a couple of weeks. I miss our game nights!"

There's a pause. Megan pats Neil's arm too. "You guys should come over!"

I actually nudge her foot. She looks at me. I make my lips a straight line, our sign for "please stop talking."

She squints a moment and turns back to them. "I literally think we have nothing going on tonight."

"No pressure," I add, nudging her foot again. "Oh hey, Megan. We still have to get our coffee, eh?" I stand up and tilt my head toward the counter.

She smiles and stays put. "Thank you, sweetie. I'll take my usual."

When I return, everything is the same, except different. The three of them look at me and they all have that same hollow look as if they just witnessed the dawn of the zombie apocalypse.

"Um? Here you go." I put Megan's blueberry scone and macchiato in front of her, plus napkins. These simple things. I set my cappuccino with my turkey and brie sandwich at my own place, which is a corner of the table.

When I sit down Megan puts her hand on mine. "Neil has cancer."

Well, now. That is different. We think we know things, but in fact, other things are true.

Neil nods. I see it now. They haven't been arguing at all. He had to lay this diagnosis on Rashmi. He feels guilt, probably. Or shame.

I shake my head. "Oh. That's terrible, Neil. Damn, I'm sorry."

Rashmi sits up straight. "We're going to beat it, though. Neil is the fighting type."

"Of course he is. Damn straight." I blow on my coffee and take a sip, which feels incongruous and frivolous in the face of a grave diagnosis.

Megan smiles. "We're having a picnic in May."

I almost spit out my coffee. I scream inside my head, "Are you serious right now?" People are dealing with cancer here, and we invite them to a picnic?

"It's going to be a beautiful day," Megan continues, as if she has a crystal ball and can predict the future. "We'll set out a big, checkered cloth and bring French bread and cheese. And a nice Chardonnay. You should come."

Neil and Rashmi both nod thoughtfully, their minds elsewhere. May is a long time away.

◆ ◆ ◆

We agree not to play games that night. Neil and Rashmi are settling with the news. But at some point in the evening, Neil calls me. "Bro?" he says.

"Dude."

I can hear him breathing. That life sound, sure and strong. "I've been thinking."

"I can only imagine."

"How come you and Megan aren't engaged or anything?"

I feel my eyebrows raise up. My mind tries to parse out why a person might bring up such a thing when they are dealing with a life-threatening disease.

"Solid question, Neil. Megan seems to wonder the same. Although… she hasn't asked about it much lately."

"Listen, Josh. We think we have so much time. All the time in the world. And we really might not."

"I see where you're going with that, buddy. I just don't have it on a timeline. If that makes sense."

"Sure. Okay. But I have to ask, is there any reason you're dragging your feet? I mean, you and Megan are awesome together. I can't imagine you with anyone else."

"Also a valid question. I will think about it, okay?"

Megan peeks into the room. I'm in the study we share. We have a deal that we can put dibs on it when one of us wants to use the computer and have some quiet time. She whispers, "Who are you talking to?"

"Neil," I whisper back.

"Please give him my love, okay?"

I nod.

"Rashmi too." She blinks as if about to cry. She remains in the doorway. Finally, she whispers, "Poor Rashmi!" And I am so taken by the tenderness of her heart and the fragility of life that my eyes tear up too.

Neil is breathing in my ear. "Still there, pardner?"

I nod again, at the phone this time. "Yep." I smile at Megan and she steps away. Then into the phone, I say, "I don't know whether to ask if you're okay. That seems like a really stupid question."

"I know. Nobody knows what to say. I'm worried about that. About you guys. And Rashmi. Other than that, I'm okay. We are starting treatment next week."

"Good." I feel glad he said 'we.' That he doesn't feel alone in this.

Neil's type of cancer is testicular, I find out a few days later. Megan seems to know everything because she has been talking to Rashmi and studying on the Internet. She informs me that only one in 5,000 people who get this kind of cancer die from it. And she says it's a treatable cancer and they don't think Neil's has spread much. But she uses the word metastasis and pronounces it "meta-stasis" like it has something to do with building a website. She also gives me a stern look and tells me to check myself daily.

Her sudden concern seems absurd, so I joke around. "You can't catch cancer, Megan. Just because Neil has it, that doesn't mean I'm next."

She hits my arm kind of hard. "Stop that."

"Ouch." I'm standing in the bedroom, putting on my tie. It's the blue one with the little pink poodles. I work in banking, and we have to wear ties to work.

She frowns. "That tie is going to get you fired."

"No one's going to fire anyone over a poodle tie."

"Or at least it will limit your advancement."

She is talking to me like we are a married couple. Or like this is how it will be if we get married. I know that a lot of couples would be engaged by now. It's the expected and normal thing. Paradigmatic. A duty, perhaps. I snug the tie up to my neck, feeling a wave of defiance. "Even bankers can have a sense of humor."

She snorts, which makes me laugh. I'm reminded that we had a whole lot more fun before marriage became the elephant in the room. I kiss her on the cheek and head to the kitchen for coffee. Then I realize there's no time for that because my bus is coming in four minutes. "Shit."

But Megan already has hot coffee for me in a travel mug, plus a little sack with a bagel and cream cheese. I suddenly feel so grateful for this thoughtful gesture that I pick her up in my arms and twirl her around. When I set her down to grab my briefcase and breakfast, she looks flushed and happy.

I need to do this more. I need to lift her up more. Figuratively, I mean. "See you tonight. How about I order pizza?"

She touches her cheek. "Okay."

We are a lucky couple. A normal couple, leading normal lives.

The ride to downtown Minneapolis on the express bus is like every other one I've ever taken. The frozen landscape passes by. There are small houses, low industrial buildings, and strip malls all the way through Hopkins and St. Louis Park. People are walking dogs that are wearing sweaters. And yet everything is different. It's like the world is a slightly different color today, or the tilt is a little off because over the weekend I found out my friend has cancer.

At the bank, I consider talking to Roger, the older banker I work with. I might mention Neil and his disease. It seems like a thing you could talk about at work, like something you don't want rattling around in your head. But I decide it feels disrespectful to talk about it.

There are meetings and I have to write up a loan for a couple younger than myself buying their first house. They both wear wedding rings, and she has a noticeable bump. I thank the stars that Megan doesn't see this. Even so, I feel her eyes on me, wondering and watchful, unsure of my intentions.

At ten o'clock I take a coffee break and check my phone. There's a text from Neil. It's just a meme with Dwight from The Office that says: "Lazy people fact #27591439: You were too lazy to read that number." I laugh. Also, I get it. He's telling me that just because he has cancer, it doesn't mean we can't laugh anymore.

I look for a Dwight meme to send back. There's one that says "FALSE. Posting to Facebook would be impossible if you were dead." I feel a bout of heart palpitations coming on. Finally, I find one where Dwight says, "I'll be honest. It doesn't hurt to be good looking." I send him that, even though it's dumb.

A new text pops up from Megan. "I was thinking about the picnic. We should serve strawberries. They will be in season."

I take a deep breath and let it go. I calculate that it is approximately 140 days until the picnic and wonder how I will survive this. I text back, "That sounds awesome."

◆　◆　◆

Neil is scheduled for surgery. It's the first step in the treatment, and I feel a little lightheaded thinking about the whole thing because they have to operate down *there*. But Megan makes me go to the hospital and buy a teddy bear in the gift shop and wait together with her and Rashmi until Neil is in recovery. Poor Neil. Emasculated and getting a teddy bear, all on the same day.

When he's conscious, he smiles at us. He doesn't seem up to holding a bear, so I set it on the bedside table. Neil has a weak voice and doesn't say much. We all talk quietly as if we're in a library or a church. When the nurse comes in speaking at a normal volume, we all look at her like she's a bull in a China shop.

"He's going to need rest," she says to us in a voice that could peel paint. Rashmi gets to stay longer because she is his wife. But we take the hint and say our goodbyes.

Megan grasps Neil's hand gently. "Get better soon."

I wave, in this nonchalant way that makes me feel like a shithead, and say, "Later, man. Take it easy."

Outside, the cold air is startling. I begin shaking all over as if I just took the polar plunge. Even when we get in the car and turn on the heat, my teeth chatter and I can't keep them from clicking together.

"Are you okay, Josh?"

I nod. "Y-y-y-yeah. Just c-c-c-cold."

"I'm putting you to bed."

I will not be ordered around, I say, but only in my head.

And in fact when we get home Megan puts me to bed. She piles on an extra comforter, and when she asks if that's enough, I tell her I need one more. Three days pass before

I can safely get out of bed without help because I'm so ill and feverish and cannot stand long enough to walk to the kitchen for a glass of water. It's not until the fever wears off that I wonder what I would have done if I had lived alone. I also realize I can't remember the last time Megan asked if we should be talking about marriage.

◆　◆　◆

Neil starts chemo treatment, and we all go into suspended animation. We don't schedule game nights because he usually doesn't feel up to doing much.

I have questions, and Megan seems to get that I don't know what's appropriate to ask. She reports that Neil's cancer was borderline stage 3 and that they found it was more extensive than they hoped. But they are fairly optimistic that he can beat it. I try to be relieved, but I have that feeling you get when you're not sure if people are just telling you what you want to hear.

I visit Neil and he seems okay and yet hollower, like someone who has lost himself. We do crosswords or play Go Fish or checkers. He works part-time as he feels up to it, and he tells me that his coworkers on the IT team at his job like to joke that he will go to any length just to get out of work.

Finally, in April, the winter thaws, and the snow and ice give way to a blank, dull landscape, leafless trees, dead grass, and mud. And that's when Megan begins to talk about the picnic in earnest.

She shows me pictures of different kinds of sandwiches on Pinterest, and crafty things we can do to make the picnic more festive. The circled date on the calendar is still four weeks away.

"Look at that." I point to the screen, standing behind her in our study. "There are red, white, and blue place settings. And a cute holder for sparklers. That's super spiffy looking."

She gives me a look as if I've just farted. "Don't be ridiculous, Josh. The picnic is in May."

I feel oddly attached to the Independence Day motif. "Well heck, we've waited this long for the picnic. What's another month and a half?"

"I don't think so. We've been planning this picnic since January."

For a moment I'm speechless. I don't understand her. I don't get why she cooked up the notion of a picnic in the dead of winter. I don't get what is so important about the end of May. And the idea that *we* have been planning this thing since January is ludicrous because it was her idea all along. Instead of biting my tongue, like always, I let it out.

"Megan, we have not been planning this picnic since January. You have. If I was going to plan a picnic, I'd wake up one morning in spring when the sun was shining and say 'Wow, it looks like a fine day for a picnic!' Then I would throw some supplies in a backpack and hike out the Winchell trail and eat a sandwich."

She blinks. Then she sits up straighter. "No one's stopping you, Josh. Go ahead. You take your picnic and I'll take mine. In fact, let's make that plan. That will make everything much easier."

"What is that supposed to mean?"

"Oh, nothing at all. But I have to plan my life." And if you think I'm going to wait around for you forever, you've got another thing coming."

"Waiting? I didn't know you were doing any waiting."

"You know what May is, Josh? Do you?" She gets up from the computer and jabs at the wall calendar with her forefinger. "It's three years since we started dating. Three years. But we're not 'dating' anymore and I don't even know what this is. I'm 26 years old. It's time for me to figure some things out."

She walks through the apartment, grabbing her cell phone and her purse from the kitchen counter and her jacket from the coat hook. I watch as she moves away from me, her long hair swishing behind her like the tail of a wild pony. Then the door slams and she's gone.

I look around the quiet apartment. The TV is on for some reason, with the sound low, the way an old man might have it if he just wants the boob tube on for company. The thought is so disturbing that I turn it off. Then I too leave the apartment, not even knowing where I'm going.

My first thought is to head over to Tuttle's and see if I can find a bowling group I can butt into. I think of a cold beer and maybe a Twins Game on in the bar, and the total awesomeness of a Saturday all to myself. Then I realize I won't enjoy it. Not with Megan mad at me. I think maybe she has gone to our favorite coffee shop. But I pull into the parking lot and can see that she's not there. Rashmi's car is there, though, so I park.

"Hey, guys." I pull up a chair and sit down. They are at the exact same table as that day they revealed the news to us. "How are you kids doing?"

Neil looks gaunt to me. He must have lost 25 or 30 pounds through all this. There's an untouched muffin in front of him. I can tell he feels like shit. But he smiles. "Pretty good, honestly. They say the treatment is working. I'm going to get well." I look at Rashmi and see tears in her eyes.

"I always believed it, dude," I tell him. "You're made of steel." But as I say this, I feel my own eyes burning, tears threatening to invade. So I point my thumb toward the barista and turn away to get coffee.

When I return, we make a toast, holding our mugs in the air like idiots and saying "Skol!"

"Hey, by the way." I lick the cappuccino foam off the rim of my mug and set it down. "The picnic Megan's been planning? It's a few weeks away, still. But she wants it to be special. Something for us all to look forward to… you know, when the weather warms up. It would be great if you both could come."

They look at each other. "Yes," Neil says. "Of course."

Rashmi smiles broadly as if she's been invited to meet the queen. "We'd be delighted."

That evening, after a day spent apart doing our own thing, Megan comes home. She seems distant, and I let her have her space, wondering what she may have done all day. My only clues are the two small shopping bags she brought home and an aroma of spring air. I wonder if she walked around one of the lakes or spent the afternoon at the Arboretum. I don't ask.

After some time spent avoiding her altogether, I step into the doorway of the bedroom. She is brushing her long black hair. I think of forest nymphs, for some reason. Her hair is kind of magical. As I watch, she sees me and smiles. And we look at the inverted versions of each other in the mirror as if we are finally seeing our full selves for the first time. Then I smile too. I wonder if we will be okay. And I wonder what it takes to make another human being happy.

After a moment, I step closer and kiss her cheek, then her neck. She stands to face me, and I tell her I'm sorry and kiss her lips, her hair, and her face. I feel as if I might dissolve into her, that I suddenly want her. All of her. Her craziness and sweetness. The beautiful wonder that is Megan that no one else in the world could ever be.

◆ ◆ ◆

The day of the picnic is bright and warm, and we spread a blanket on the greening grass by the Lake of the Isles. Neil wears a warm jacket and seems a bit flummoxed and apologetic.

"My thermometer is all out of whack," he says, with an embarrassed smile. "But the doctor says that will get better."

Megan puts out a charcuterie board and a spectacular array of little spreads with tiny knives, warm French bread, cheeses, olives, and sliced vegetables with hummus. She hands out some charming pale green cloth napkins. I think of the Independence Day set I wanted, which seems gaudy and out of place, now. This is just right.

A couple walking a tiny puppy passes by—the woman waddling, heavy with a baby on board. The puppy suddenly breaks away and runs to us, squirming and excited and ridiculously fluffy. Rashmi, who has been lying on her side, gets puppy kisses and is lovingly mauled, and we laugh so hard it hurts.

Neil looks happy. He says to Rashmi, "Maybe we need a puppy."

Rashmi wipes off her face, still smiling. "Yes. I think we do."

The couple waves and strolls away, with their puppy bouncing after them like an animated mop. I wonder about the secret to life—to a life well lived—and what makes us whole enough to be of any use to others. I feel the ring in my pocket, in its secret box, silent and powerful. And I know we will carry on, that we will love, and we will heal. And anything is possible.

5

The Walled City

Peril was like a snake, lurking in the shadows, whispering its secret desires. Leila considered this idea, huddled in a blanket on her veranda in Lucca—4,720 miles from Minneapolis. Her coffee was hot, her laptop cold. The February sun behaved as if it would like to warm her but just couldn't muster the strength.

She looked out over the stone architecture and tiled rooftops of the walled city, contemplating the future. The year had started off promising. The year 2020 wasn't just a new year. It was a new decade. And she had just begun a new life, jettisoning her crumbling past for a new start in a land known for magnificent food and lovely ruins.

But it was all tinged with doubt now. She had been watching the news for weeks, the way a sailor looks out to sea at an oncoming storm. The Coronavirus outbreak had traveled west from Asia into Europe, tagging along with business travelers and vacationers like a parasite. Perhaps it was no longer safe in Europe. This… thing… whatever it was… seemed to be moving fast, even with flights to and from China suspended. What if it couldn't be contained?

The sounds of sleep-drugged muttering emerged from the bedroom inside the flat.

"Come back to bed!"

Matteo, the exquisite, fawn-eyed local she had taken up with, worked nights in a restaurant and she never knew when he would wake in the morning—ravenous, but not for food.

They were compatible in most things, she and Matteo. The virus, however, was an ongoing argument. He tended to wave his hand at the contagion reports, the way one bats at a pesky mosquito.

"It's just another media circus," he said, with a tone that straddled wry and sarcastic. "Do you know how many ads they sell because of this? Don't feed the machine."

The argument was silly, because disagreements were for relationships that are serious, and this totally wasn't. And so, a brush of those lips on her cheek or spine was all it took to forgive him.

To keep the peace, she only peeked at the news when he was at work or sleeping. It was changing day by day. In January, the talk was all about Wuhan. Containment. Border security. It seemed as if it could all get figured out. But a month later, outbreaks were popping up every-where.

A loud yawn came from the bedroom, ending in "Lei-LAAA!"

Swaddled in her blanket against the chill of the Feb-ruary morning, she called back, "No, my love. I've got a coffee and it's so beautiful out here. Birds are singing." In truth, there were only pigeons, and their sad little coos re-flected her pensiveness. It was too cold in February for many of the other birds.

She bit a nail and spit it over the railing, then contin-ued glancing quickly through Time, Bloomberg, CNN. And then she saw it. A BBC report. It said the cases in Italy had suddenly jumped from 80 to 400, just in the last few days. This set off little explosions of fear in her mind. The article reported that 12 people had now died in Italy.

She sat with that information, swallowing the last of the coffee. Twelve people was not very many out of 400, was it? And 400 was but a drop in the bucket in a population of over 60 million. Right?

What a time to be unmoored. An expatriate. Back in Minnesota, it would be the middle of the night. People would be tucked into bed after bedtime stories and night caps. Everyone she had thrown away—Richard (ex-husband), Nancy (ex-sister), and Timothy (her nephew, the proverbial baby that went out with the bathwater) was in bed, dreaming the dreams of contented people.

She could hear Nancy's voice, resonating long after the one phone conversation that had transpired between them since she left. "So, you've found yourself an Italian stallion!"

Bitch.

Still, she ached for home a little. Would they worry? Would anyone call? No. She had gotten a one-way ticket here, shutting the door on all of it. But it didn't matter. Nothing mattered except Timothy, her sweet boy, as much a part of her as her fingertips and eyelashes. She imagined him in sleep, the teddy bears lining his bed. His Star Wars night light glowing softly in the corner, warding off the monsters.

How had she lost him?

She had run—that was how. She'd run from the liars and traitors who had ripped her marriage apart and had enclosed herself in this walled city. For a while, she believed nothing could touch her here.

"I will stalk you like a lion," Matteo called from the bed.

"Coming my love!" She closed the laptop and swished back to the bedroom in her blanket gown with the February sun streaming in the high windows like the light of angels, and Pavarotti singing Celeste Aida as only a booming Italian tenor could.

♦　♦　♦

That afternoon, she strolled into town, meandering through cobbled streets. A pigeon ran in front of her, fluttered up onto a wall and pecked at something. She heard distant chimes emanating from a bell tower, sounding ancient and desultory. Then she entered the busy area where taxis whooshed, and gray filmy smog belched from diesel trucks. Everything seemed so normal.

She looked at her watch. Timothy would be eating breakfast.

At the bakery, she scanned the bread selection. Giada, who was a goddess at upselling, smiled and indicated a fresh pastry that emanated the aromas of yeast and cinnamon. Leila and Giada rarely exchanged words. Instead, they pointed, wrote out numbers in the flour dusting the counter, and occasionally used the limited vocabulary one reserves for simple people and children. Such was the language barrier.

She wanted to ask Giada, "What have you heard about the virus? Is it coming here?" But there was no use. Even English-speaking people didn't seem to know much about it or thought perhaps the journalists were making it up. She had spoken to a couple from Iowa who insisted it was a money scheme. "Mark my words," the man said, "Big pharma is behind this. They'll come out with a vaccine or a treatment or what have you. We'll all have to get poked, and they'll get rich."

She shrugged. What did she know of these things? Conspiracy theorists seemed to have been coming out of the woodwork in recent years, emboldened by people actually listening to them.

Giada gave a sad farewell wave, as Leila stepped toward the door with her single loaf of bread. Was that sad demeanor about the cinnamon cake?

She stepped into the sunshine with her small parcel and moved down the street to the meat shop. She would need something more than bread for her handsome inamorato. The butcher was sharpening a knife against a stone with a swish, swish motion. He wore a fresh apron, and it glowed blindingly white in the sunlight splashing off the stainless-steel counter. She stared at the hanging lamb and veal carcasses and smelled the aromas of meat and blood.

The butcher set down his knife. "The lamb is very fresh, Leila. So fresh, you might hear it bah-bahing to you."

His name was Daniel, and he had an almost startling lack of an accent in both Italian and English. She had learned one day that he had earned a Poli Sci degree at UCLA, graduating with honors. And then he returned home to Lucca. He told her, "I knew then I could do whatever I wanted, and that's what mattered. Turns out I wanted to be here, with these easy-going people in this bustling town, where in springtime we feast and in summer we swim in the sea. Anyway, politics is rife with idiots and egotists. Who needs it?"

Now she peered into the meat case. "I'd like something small. It's just for two. Nothing still bahing or mooing, please."

He nodded, a knowing look on his face. "Lamb is the most romantic of meats. It is as if it lives on, its zest for life so spectacular that mere death cannot contain it."

"Are you sure you didn't study poetry?" She thought of Matteo and felt her color rising.

"I may have taken a literature elective. We Italians are romantic, you know. Just tell me when you want me to recite a poem."

"Of course."

As he cut the lamb shanks, she asked him about the virus. Or rather, she dropped a casual mention the way a lady may have dropped a kerchief in the old days. "So," she said. "That virus is starting to seem menacing. I read today that 400 people have become sick, just here in this country. And 12 have died."

"Oh, don't you worry," he said. He wrapped the meat in paper and sealed the parcel with tape. "It's the older people. The infirm. Sad, yes, but it's just like the flu. Every year, we lose some vulnerable people."

She wanted to believe that this denial of what seemed to be coming their way would somehow protect them, as if Armageddon could occur all around them, and they would be just fine—protected by the walls of Lucca.

"But Daniel," she said. "There were over 300 people diagnosed in just one day." She was telling him this not to convince him, but because she hoped to be mollified. His bright intelligent eyes and confident voice reassured her, almost regardless of what he might say. Just keep talking, she thought.

"Yes, yes. There's bound to be a spike. We have no immunity to this virus. Especially those who are frail." He looked into her eyes. "I can see how you are, Miss Leila. You are the worrying type. And you know what they say about worry?"

She shook her head and took the package he handed to her. "No, what do they say?"

"My friend, they say if you worry then you suffer twice. Once for things that may or may not happen, and then again when something finally does."

"Thank you, Daniel," she said. But she was thinking that there were worse things than only suffering two times.

At the outdoor market she picked up fruit and cheese, then she sat on a park bench to eat her lunch and was befriended by a tiny flock of pigeons. The day was not quite warm, and she longed for spring. In March, warmer days would come. The pall would lift. Perhaps with more people outdoors, there would be less infection.

Back home in Minneapolis, it was still the dead-of-winter. Snow everywhere. Lakes frozen solid and covered with ice fishing houses and SUVs. Maybe the cold would keep Timothy safe. No one travels to Minnesota in the winter unless they have to.

Here the people seemed to be lying in wait and dread, the way a dog will wince against anger or abuse but will not run away. Was this what it was like for the poor civilians in the towns and villages across Europe in the war, who never thought Hitler's armies would come? But they did. They rolled through in tanks, killing off whole villages, or requisitioning their food and supplies and leaving them to starve.

Could this be something like that? Everyone trapped by denial, while just beyond lay the inevitability of it all?

Here in this Tuscan light, one could pretend anything. There were pigeons and bell towers, the buzz of scooters, people on bicycles delivering packages and a general sense that nothing could ever go terribly wrong.

Evening came. Leila roasted the lamb with potatoes and rosemary and ate with Matteo by candlelight. Soon he would go to work.

She was again startled by his beauty, almost nervously so, as if to breathe deeply was to risk blowing his apparition away. He had that Roman nose, those high cheeks, and full lips that could have put him in good stead as a sculptor's model. His dark curls bobbed on his head as they talked over the meal. He would be pulling his hair back into a ponytail on his way out the door, inadvertently flexing his biceps, a gesture that made her weak.

"It's going to be slow," he said, after a sip of Barolo. "This fucking virus has everyone spooked. More people are staying home."

She sipped from her own glass, contemplating life and the murderous and magnificent turns of events throughout history. When was the fall of the Roman Empire? When did Michelangelo carve the statue of David?

"That must be awful."

"It is. The general manager turns into a beast, because of course there go the profits. This damn thing could go on for months."

"Or maybe it will become a global pandemic and completely alter life as we know it."

"Ah, mi amore, you and your doomsday predictions and zombie apocalypses. This will blow over."

She smirked at him. "You have such a voice of authority. I have no choice but to believe you."

On the way to the door, he pulled her to him, kissing her and then swinging her around. Then he ran his nose up her neck and kissed her all over. "Will you wait up for me?"

"I will try, my love."

She cleaned the dishes and drank more wine after he left. With Aida turned up, Pavarotti's voice seemed to expand inside the apartment, with its high ceilings and remarkable acoustics that turned the place into a symphony hall when she closed her eyes.

Just as she was drying the last dish, her phone made an odd jangling sound—and she recognized it as the peculiar ring of a Facetime call. She saw Timothy's face and dropped the dish towel to answer. "Oh hello, sweet boy!"

His face was still cherubic, with a sweep of auburn hair. Those fetching dimples that had delighted her since he was a baby still disarmingly decorated each cheek.

"Hi Aunt Leila!"

"What a surprise! To what do I owe the honor?"

"You've been gone SO long. I'm bored of waiting. When are you coming back?"

How long had it been? She'd left a week before Christmas, a time she had always loved because of the snow and magic of Minnesota. But it would have been unbearable under the circumstances. When her husband left her for her sister, time became tricky and mirage-like. A house had to be buttoned down. A plan made. A plane boarded. All through hideous, unbearable grief.

Now she realized she had allowed time to erase her footsteps, unsure of whether she could return to the past, and certain she could not plan the future.

"Well, kiddo, I don't know if they'll sell me a plane ticket. I kind of made someone mad at the airport because I lost my boarding pass. They don't take kindly to that, you know."

"You dummy!"

"I know! I am such a dum-dum!"

"Guess what."

"I am afraid to guess! You've grown up so much, maybe you're going to tell me you're growing a moustache."

"No silly. I asked Mom why you left. She says you're mad." The dimples slid away, as a cloud crossed his face. His lashes were so dark, and his eyes so bright, it gave him an elfin appearance. "Are you mad at *me*, Aunt Leila?"

"Oh baby, no. Of course not. I could never be mad at you." A time capsule opened up, and out poured a collage of their Saturday outings. Snapshots of museums in winter, and in summer the ice cream shops, the Minnesota zoo, the beaches and the arboretum. Once they had taken a trip down to Lanesboro for trout fishing. She had taught him everything she knew and then he caught two good-sized trout that cooked up well over a fire. How her heart ached.

"Guess what else," he whispered.

She whispered back, "I don't know, Buddy. What?"

"It's weird having Uncle Richard live here."

For a moment she could only press her lips together and nod. "Uncle Richard," her ex-husband, had crossed over to a new role. Liars and charlatans should never be allowed to be uncles or fathers. They should be stripped of all such rights. She did not say these things. Instead, she said, "Yeah, Buddy. I guess that would be pretty weird." She closed her eyes slowly, buying time, then looked at him again. "But…"

His eyebrows raised up, a facial gesture inherited directly from her ex-sister, Nancy. It was the equivalent of drumming fingers, and it meant, "I'm waiting!" It also meant he was growing up. She wanted to stop him, to keep him small, but knew she lacked that kind of power.

"Well," she ventured. "I guess you could say he's not really your uncle anymore. Right? I mean, now that he's married to your mom and not to me, he's your stepdad. Maybe you could think of him that way." Leila shrugged, hoping to dull the impact of her words, but she could see they were all wrong.

He shook his head, his eyes glistening. "No," he said, sniffing. "My dad died. I don't need another dad. That's all I have to say about that."

"That's alright, Buddy. I'm sure Richard doesn't mind being your uncle, like forever."

He blinked, and the tears stopped, and the dimples came back. "Yeah, but my friend Bobby says he's a douche."

Leila covered her mouth, trapping a laugh. "Timothy, I'm going to pretend you didn't just say that."

"Sorry, Auntie. I better go. I have homework."

She wanted to keep hearing his voice, to hold him captive in her heart. But she said, "Okay. Bye, Buddy. I love you more than bananas!"

"I know!" he said, and for a moment she thought he had outgrown their custom. But before he clicked off, he said, "I love you more than coconuts! Please come home!" Then he was gone.

The next day, she visited the coffee shop run by her friend Serena, whom she had met in a dance class.

Kiss kiss. Serena greeted her, then clasped her by the arms and stood back. "What is it? So worried!"

"Can you tell?"

"You're only looking over your shoulder every three seconds," Serena said. "You got a stalker or something?"

Serena made them cappuccinos and asked her daughter to watch the shop. Then they sat at a small table on the sidewalk, huddled in their jackets.

"People are dying of this virus, Serena. They say it's getting worse here, fast. Those two people who died in Rome? It was just the beginning." Already this felt like old news. The morning had come and gone without so much as a peek at her laptop. Matteo had awakened with her, pulling her down into his arms when she tried to get up to make coffee, and that was that.

Serena drank from her cappuccino and licked the foam from her lips. "Good news, darling. No one comes to Lucca unless they have to."

Leila smiled, wanting to let down her guard. She wanted to hear that the worst was over. Meanwhile, she would make do with cappuccino and comfort.

"Oh," Serena said. "Did you hear about the quarantine in Lombardy?"

"What?"

"Yes. Some guy who was sick went around seeing all these people and didn't take any care whatsoever. They say it's like a bomb going off. Dozens and dozens of people infected, and then they are going around infecting more. They've quarantined whole cities."

"Oh my God."

"It's not good. But I guess maybe the quarantine will help."

"Lombardy? How far is that?"

Serena laughed at Leila's lack of geographic sensibilities. Then she formed Italy on the table with a sugar dispenser and napkins. "This is Tuscany," she said, pointing to the north coast. She slid her finger inland. "This is Lombardy. And this is Lucca. We are close neighbors."

Leila put her hand to her mouth. "But… here? In Italy? Why here?"

"Sweetie, you know as much as I know now. Oh, except they are saying to wear masks, and yet you can't find them anywhere. So… people are sewing them."

"Thank you. I've got to get going. I need to get something for the evening meal and head back. The coffee was lovely."

They air kissed again, and then she left for the shops. As she walked toward Daniel's, she felt her phone vibrate. It was a text from her ex-sister Nancy, and it was only one line. "Leave my son alone."

She stopped, then, to lean against the side of a stone fountain, nearly unable to breathe. All around her, life carried on. Scooters buzzed past, sometimes with two riders, talking to one another and laughing over the sound of the engine. There were city buses, taxis and cars all motoring by, so orderly, so normal. And along the city wall, people strolled and held hands or biked or pushed strollers, a Twilight Zone of unreal reality. Maybe the virus really was a hoax. Even her husband leaving her for her own sister—the very one now telling her to stay away from Timothy—seemed like a joke gone wrong. None of this could be real.

Pigeons scuttled aside as she walked to Daniel's shop, her feet carrying her though she wasn't sure for what purpose. To buy food to cook and eat? What was the point of these frivolous acts? But when she entered the shop, Daniel was not there. Some other man stood there in Daniel's place, wearing a bloodied white apron and making cuts of meat.

A zombie. She blinked. No, just a man—one with an impressive likeness to her friend.

She stood in the doorway until he raised his eyebrows in greeting. Then he returned to his work. When she didn't move, he looked up. "May I help you?"

"Where is Daniel?" Even as she asked the question, she knew she didn't want the answer. She shook her head, begging him not to say it.

"He is ill, my friend. I'm his brother. Just here to help keep things running until he's back on his feet."

"How ill?"

"Some kind of flu. But say a prayer, nonetheless. It never hurts." He crossed himself. "He'll be fine. I'm quite sure."

It was the beginning of the end. She knew it as certain as she had ever known anything.

An hour later, her bags were packed. She stood facing Matteo, unable to say whatever needed to be said. This had come too soon. He pulled her to him, his arms completely enclosing her. How she loved the feel of those strong arms around her.

"Why must you go?" His eyes were wet with tears. "I am falling for you, mi amore."

She closed her eyes. Held him. Breathed in his cologne. "I think I fell for you long ago, my love. But things are turning bad here. I don't want to leave. But I need to get back home for now. There's a little boy I absolutely must see. I need to know he's okay."

"A child?"

"Yes. My nephew." She realized she had never told him any of this. Or why she was here. It was too late, though. And there was too much to tell. "Come with me. Maybe we can outrun this together."

But he smiled and shook his head. "No. My life is here. Just come back to me when this is over. I'll be waiting."

Then she received a text that her Uber driver had arrived. "I have to go, Matteo."

He walked her out and helped to load her bags in the car, their time together reduced to logistics. He held her, kissed her hair, breathing into her ear, "Goodbye, mi amore."

She climbed into the car and waved as her car pulled away, leaving Matteo to grow smaller and smaller before the car turned a corner and he disappeared like a candle snuffing out.

Transatlantic flights had already proven to be the perfect opportunity to descend into the cesspool of her mind. It would have been survivable if she could sleep. But she could not. A baby cried from time to time, and someone coughed almost incessantly. The flight attendants seemed nervous and skittish as wild animals, something she had never seen before. One wore a surgical mask, which looked ridiculous. But Leila entertained the possibility that everyone would be wearing them before long.

She daydreamed of home. Her forever-ago first home, when she and Nancy were young, and living in what would appear to anyone as a storybook life. Their family had land and stables and horses, just outside the sprawl of suburbs that continually crept further and further west from Minneapolis. They each had a pony. Hers was named Sugar and Nancy's was Maple.

Perhaps she could have seen what was to come, back then. Sugar was the good horse, Nancy said, indicating that the system was rigged. Maple was a kicker. You couldn't venture anywhere near that hind end. She would back away obstinately as Nancy tried to bridle her. And sometimes she would bite. Leila suspected it was all in how Nancy handled her and that a firm, but soothing voice would make all the difference. But you couldn't suggest things to Nancy. That was just not done.

Leila remembered realizing one day how she and Nancy each carried after one parent. Nancy had assumed the attitude of the surly and self-righteous, an odd carbon copy of their father. Meanwhile, Leila was like their mother. Demure. Neurotic. She even had the same slight features as if they were just naturally paired with insecurity.

No one greeted her on the ground. Who even knew where she was? No one, except far away Matteo. The thought of him made her heart feel brittle, like chipped ice. Perhaps he had already begun the process of letting go. She bundled up the best she could against the brutal Minnesota cold, and then bookended her flight with another Uber ride, this time across the frozen landscape to her closed-up home. Her key was where she always kept it, in the mouth of a stone frog just under the eaves near the dormant garden.

Then suddenly, startlingly, she was inside her shuttered ghost home, which seemed to release a sigh of melancholy. Amidst the chores of turning up the heat, opening blinds, starting a pot of coffee, and removing sheets from furniture, she paused to text one word back to Nancy. "Why?"

Though she didn't expect a response, she was not letting the sun set with her unspoken declaration clawing at her heart—that she outright refused to give up everything she loved. That there was no more she could give. No. This word rolled over in her mind as she showered and drank her coffee.

But then she winced when an answer came. "He's stressed. He doesn't understand. I don't want you upsetting him."

Her Mini Cooper hesitated, then came to life on the second try. In a few moments, she was on her way over the icy streets, shivering, with the heater turned up. Past a frozen lake, covered with its encampments of ice houses, sun shining bright on the snow, conjuring memories of happy Christmases.

Finally, she pulled up and parked near her ex-sister's enormous gray bungalow with its circular drive, white pillars, and sleeping fountain. She had to see Timothy. No matter what. As she walked up the driveway toward the house, she was determined to make this quite clear.

That was when she felt it. An awareness that something was not right. That she had not been feeling well since she stepped off the plane. A deep ache had begun settling into her bones. Perhaps it was just the long flight. But no, there was a kind of heat rising in her too. A burning. She thought of the coughing man on the plane. Of Daniel. The outbreak in nearby Lombardy. And her walled city, which was incapable of keeping anything out or in.

And she knew. She had brought the illness here with her, like extra baggage.

Her feet were still moving, as if by uncontrolled momentum, and she stopped. Before her were the two solid white double doors that opened to a world where her nephew played, did his homework, watched T.V. and fell asleep by the glow of a light saber. She stepped away.

Timothy's room was on the second floor at the back. "Please be there," she thought, as she skirted the house. She pulled the ladder from its hooks on the side of the shed and quietly set it against the house next to Timothy's window. Then she climbed, rung by rung. The body aches seemed to intensify with each step.

At the top, she peered through icicles that crusted the windowpane. He was lying stomach-down on his bed, reading a book, moving his feet lazily in the air. She tapped gently on the window. When he looked up, she pressed a finger to her lips. Eyes wide, he came to her, and tried to open the window, but she shook her head. She pressed her finger to her lips again, afraid of him making any sound at all.

In his little boy eyes, she saw hope and sadness, but there was something else too. It was mischief. The love of adventure. The wonder at this amazing thing—that his auntie would climb a ladder just to see him.

She wished she had brought a letter, so she could tell him everything. But so much was still unknown. How did the virus spread? By air or by touch?

She took off her glove and placed her hand flat against the glass. From the other side, Timothy pressed his hand against hers. They smiled and she mouthed the words "I love you more than bananas." And he mouthed, "I love you more than coconuts."

She pulled her fingers from the cold pane, and for a moment she pretended the glove was trying to slap her face. Timothy laughed, and his eyes sparkled in a magical reflection of winter light. But it was so cold. She put her glove back on, shivering, hot and aching. Then she blew Timothy a kiss and waved to let him know she was leaving.

He waved solemnly, the sparkle in his eyes turning to mist, to longing. He picked up one of his bears, made it dance for her, then held it close.

Finally, she stepped back down the ladder, rung by rung by rung, as alone as she had ever been—yet fortified and whole. Ready to face the unknown.

The peculiar serenity of Lake Superior is one reason I've come. To behold its reflective surface that can turn sullen and angry like a monster and swallow boats whole when its mood shifts. We had many storms when I was a child. One time, three boats were sucked into its dark depths, taking 11 sailors, including my friend Emily's father who was a fisherman. I remember how he could gut and clean a fish in about the same amount of time it took me to brush my teeth.

I remember it all. The ships out on the horizon, hauling lumber and ore. The chill air that rises off the lake and seems to slip into your skin like a spirit. How, as a child, I played on the shore with my friends when the weather was calm, and ran home when the storms rolled in.

"Jules," my mother calls. But she is not there. I hear her calling me home, just like in the old days, when she would stand on our porch as I played in the storm debris with the neighbor children. That is the other reason I have come here—back to the place I was born, where I came of age. It is time to see about the house and all the collected things of my mother's lifetime.

I look down the old rough road and see people stopping into shops. It's just past tourist season and our harbor town has gone quiet except for the retirees who have nothing but time. Little has changed.

There was an old machine shop not far from the edge of the lake that was both industrious and enigmatic. The proprietor, a man of wizened but indeterminate age, used to give us candy.

Thinking about that place, I realize it had a role in who I became—a silver jeweler—forever trying to shape things. I momentarily hear its harsh sounds of metal, of machines turning and grinding. But it is drowned out by the call of the gulls, talking to me.

It seems they are shrieking about something on the beach. I look and see a bulky heap on the sand. It is gray and unmoving, about a football field away.

I stare at the form, not certain what I am seeing. Here on Minnesota's North Shore, we are scavengers, eager for excitement that rarely comes. So I look around because when anything washes up on shore, it inevitably draws a crowd. But there is no one.

I set out at a trot, wanting to be the first to see it, to claim it as my own find. When I get to it, I can see that it is human-sized. Human shaped. But unrecognizable.

A seagull is standing on it, as if this is the only dry land for miles around. I shoo it away and bend down. There is hair. Quite a lot of hair. And a swollen gray surface that must have been skin. The body has been tossed by the waves and rolled across the sand. It is mangled, wadded, like wet, dirty socks. And I can make out nothing more without touching it.

So I do touch it. Not the face. Not the skin. I'm not braced for that. I pull at its fabric covering. The body appears to be intentionally wrapped, like a spider's prey. I imagine sailors wrapping and tossing it off a ship to bury it at sea—or, in this case, into the waters of Lake Superior.

Then I find a pocket in the fabric, and I realize that it is not some kind of burial wrapping, but a weatherproof parka. The pocket is empty. I peel back an edge of the coat, and see another inner pocket with a closed zipper, and tug it. The zipper resists, clotted with sand, then comes open.

I reach in, hoping to find some kind of identification. Instead, my hand grasps something cold, metallic. I bring it out. It is a key that has started to rust. I close my hand around it to warm it. That is when I hear voices down the beach, asking if everything is alright. It is an elderly couple in jogging suits.

"There's been an accident," I tell them. "We need to call the… authorities." I cannot think what kind of emergency services are appropriate for this. Ambulances are for the injured. Police officers are for law enforcement. And firefighters are for fires. So….

"The woman leans forward. Not too close. As if the body might spring to life. "Oh! Yes. I'm afraid it may be Mr. Hess."

"You know him?"

"Yes," the woman says. "Everyone knows Duncan Hess." She looks down, dabs at her nose. "He's… been missing since last Saturday when he took his trawler out. The wind came up that afternoon and whipped up the lake. We've all feared the worst."

The man appraises me. "You're not from around here." His arms are folded. He glances at the body, as if he can't look, but can't look away.

"Oh I am," I say, rising from my crouched position. "Or, I was. My mother was Clare Benson, from over on Lake Street. I'm Julie. I grew up here."

The man nods, his skepticism easing. "I'm Adam. This is Rose. We moved here when we retired."

Rose steps away from the body. "We're just over there," she says, pointing to the senior living condos that went up a few years ago. "We'll call the sheriff."

The moment is awkward. Am I to go with them? Or stay here alone with the body? I've begun to feel a chill. I can't look at Mr. Hess any longer, and have lost the weird desire to claim him as my find.

I see Rose absorb all of this. "There's no point in you waiting here. Where are you staying? In case the sheriff wants to talk with you."

I explain that I'm in town to close up my mother's house, and provide the street address. I look again at the swollen lump of cloth and hair and sand that was Mr. Hess. My lips are quivering—from cold, perhaps. Or shock. "Thank you. I'll go, then."

We part and head down the beach in opposite directions. The gulls call overhead as if I've missed something.

At home, I find the key, still clutched in my hand. Dread and sorrow wash over me. I begin to formulate an explanation for the sheriff. Night is coming on. A team will be busy with extracting the body, dealing with the coroner. Will they contact me today? Should I explain about the key?

I set it on the counter near my mother's ancient, stained Mr. Coffee machine. Then I pick it up again and put it under one of her crocheted doilies. I don't want to see it.

I spot a phone directory near her telephone. Everyone still has a landline in this town, even in 2019, because cell phone reception is abysmal.

Duncan Hess is easy to find in the directory. He lives only three blocks away. My mother must have known him. Everywhere her aroma of mildew, dust and hyacinth perfume linger.

"What are you doing?" her apparition asks.

I wave her away. "I don't know." Dusk has fallen. Shadows linger and sway in the light of area lamps. The dim lighting vaguely illuminates the stacks of boxes I've begun filling with donation items. "I'll figure this out."

Ricky speaks to me next. "Hon," he says, as if we are still together and he still possesses some part of me. "You need to do something with that key."

"Yes. I know. And if you weren't a cheating bastard, you'd be here right now. I wouldn't be figuring this out alone."

In my mother's cupboard I find baking soda and a bottle of white vinegar. I take out a dish and drop the key in. I cover it with baking soda. I pour in the vinegar and watch while it eats the rust away. At any moment I expect a knock at the door. Instead, the hall clock ticks and ticks.

I wash and dry the key. At last the phone rings, shattering the ugly silence.

"Hello, Ms. Benson? Sheriff Larson."

"Good evening, Sheriff." I think about Mr. Hess. A death in the community. I wonder how old he was. If he was married. "I'm sorry about…" My voice trails off. "I mean, was it Mr. Hess?"

"That's pending investigation. He had no local family. No next of kin for identification. So…." He trails off. Does he think I'm too delicate to hear the word *autopsy*?

"I see. What can I do for you?"

"Not much, I'm afraid. But please tell us what you saw. From the beginning."

"I took a walk to the lake in the late afternoon, to take a break from housework. And that's when I saw him. He seemed to have just… washed up there. There's nothing more to tell."

"Thank you for your time, Ms. Benson. If we have any further questions, we'll be in touch."

When he hangs up, I look at the key. It is clean now, and shiny in the kitchen light.

I put on my coat, grab a flashlight from the utility closet, and leave the house. It is dark and the gulls have gone quiet. I hear the lapping of waves from the lake on the shore, as I walk the few blocks to Mr. Hess's home.

His house sits on a good-sized lot. A small garden borders the weathered bungalow, and it is decorated with a lake theme—enormous bobbers, floats, an anchor, a mermaid statue, and another of a seagull. I look in the windows all around, seeing nothing but the hulking shapes of furniture, before trying the key at the back door. It turns easily and I enter the dark house, quietly closing the door behind me.

I turn my flashlight on low beam, and keep it focused on the floor. Just enough to see by, but not to be seen. The shadows beyond its circle-glow are deep.

"Hello?"

No answer. Though I am used to hearing from the living and the dead, it is not my choosing when it will be.

The house is tidy. Mr. Hess kept things in order. A small desk with a computer sits in one corner of the living room. There is a TV. An easy chair. Magazines about fishing and lake life on an end table.

I am looking for something and I don't know what. But I sense it is here. I close my eyes. I open them again. A curtain stirs. A shadow passes.

"Mr. Hess?"

No answer.

Something is moving in the room. Along the floor. Coming toward me. I drop my flashlight. I bend quickly to retrieve it. I shine it toward the movement.

A cat.

"Oh!" I say. "It's just you."

At last Mr. Hess speaks. "Her name is Sasha," he says.

I nod at this. She is small and gray. Elegant, and perfectly named.

As she winds around my legs, and lets me pick her up, I think of my mother, and a cat named Maddie that we loved when I was little. She was life and warmth. To this day, I treasure a picture of her sitting in our living room window, looking out at a stormy day. We buried her in a shoebox, with a white stone to mark her grave. We said we could never own another cat.

"It's time," my mother says.

I understand. It is time to stitch the present to the past. To cast off shadow and doubt. To release our earthly clutter. To shout memories into the lake's expanse where they can be swallowed up like wayward souls.

"I will take care of her, Mr. Hess."

I feel him smile. And he too moves on, for there is no reason for either of us to remain here in this house.

Author's note: Cast Off was first published in June, 2023 in Great Lakes Review.

7

Hiding in Plain Sight

In her 34 years, Delia had been many things—an entrepreneur, a writer, a cook, and a wife, to name a few—none of them and all of them leading her here to a homeless encampment under a bridge spanning the Mississippi River in June. She could see the lights of Minneapolis and St. Paul, glowing prisms of wonder and wealth, like diamonds glimmering in a mine.

The bridge offered some shelter, and that was good. And she was not alone.

A rough woman's voice spoke nearby. "Ya want some eggs?"

Delia had emerged from her tent and had not yet thought of her first move of the day. There were birds flitting in and out of nests in the bridge's support beams, and she wondered what they were. Starlings? Swallows? She recognized the woman who stood holding a frying pan in a gnarled hand as the one who lived in the faded green tent near the water.

"Eggs?" Delia asked, as if it was a trick question.

"Here," the woman said. "I have extra." And with that, the woman handed Delia a paper plate, and then scraped some eggs onto it with a broken wooden spoon.

Delia nodded, amazed by this tender act of kindness. "Thank you. It smells very good." Her stomach rumbled like a far-off storm.

There were no seasonings and no cutlery. She had not thought of these things yet. So, she sat on the rolling office chair she'd found for free at the end of a nearby driveway, folded the plate, and tipped it into her mouth. The eggs tasted like home. Like her mother's long-ago kitchen. Gardens, chickens, hope, prosperity. All in this warm, sagging plate.

When the eggs were gone, she took the plate to an overflowing trash barrel at the edge of the encampment and shoved it inside, avoiding the sight of a spent syringe. All around, others were emerging from lean-tos, tents, and plywood shelters. A woman in curlers walked a tiny hairless dog on a frayed pink leash to the edge of a piece of grass. Two teenagers—a boy and a girl—strung out and skinny, with their hair in dreadlocks, argued quietly next to a tiny humming camp stove supporting a metal coffee percolator. And at the edge of the area populated with tents and shanties, a small boy stood with his back to the people, peeing on some weeds. He had coffee-colored skin and wore mud-brown clothes, giving him the appearance of being in a sepia-toned movie. What color had his clothes once been?

She looked away, giving these people their time and their privacy. The encampment was situated in the heart of an industrial complex. She could see warehouses, shipping crates, dry docks, and a parking lot full of white trucks shining in the morning sun. A food truck with a giant ice cream cone emblazoned on its side rumbled down the bridge's off-ramp onto a surface street. Incongruously, it passed a billboard offering weight-loss services in Minneapolis.

She would need to start thinking about lunch. How did these people get food? She would wait and watch. The words required for her to ask the question were held in a limbo world of uncertainty.

The rules of camp were not written. They were not spoken. They just were. Mothers with children were given priority at the ad hoc washing station consisting of water jugs, a bar of soap and towels that were washed at a local coin-op laundry. New folks had to announce themselves to a large, grizzled man called Gerald, who acted as mayor. And at night around the fire, you were not to stare at anyone but those you were acquainted with, for direct eye contact could signal hostility. Delia surmised all these things quickly.

"You can set up over here," the mayor had said, when she arrived the day before, pushing a cart from the hardware store, her head covered with a plastic shopping bag in the drizzle of rain. She smiled and was grateful.

She had set up in the damp late afternoon. It wasn't a bad shelter, compared with some. She'd had enough cash in her purse when she left Blake to buy a tent, a sleeping bag, some cord, and some extra tarps and poles to fashion a lean-to against the wind. Was she safe? She couldn't say. Safer than with Blake, maybe.

The rain from the night before had stopped by morning. Delia saw that the others were laying out their damp things to dry in the sun. She did the same, using the rolling chair, the tent and a length of cord to extend a clothesline, where she hung out her few things to dry. Then she went into her tent to count her money where she couldn't be seen.

$42.95

In some wry part of her mind, she calculated that this was approximately $1,999,957 less than she would have if Blake died of a heart attack. Or in a tragic accident. Murder didn't count. Not if she was the perpetrator.

What would become of her now? Cold dread seeped in. She had not been able to think beyond this. Now, however, she had nothing but time. And no one to turn to. She had disappeared into a different reality from anything she had experienced or had hoped to experience in her life. It was such a bleak idea that she felt as if she was petrifying right there in her tent. Turning to stone.

Outside the tent, there was the sound of a bell ringing, and when she emerged, she saw that a small church service had begun. The minister was a thickset man with a shock of white hair that made him look intelligent and grandfatherly, like Santa and Einstein all in one. In lieu of vestments, he wore a red scarf that draped down his chest on both sides, over a faded blue t-shirt. About 10 people had pulled up camp chairs and picnic benches to hear his sermon.

Delia sat in her chair, for lack of anything better to do, and listened. The minister was saying something about hope. About never giving up.

"I shall read for you from Psalm 88," he said, as he opened a worn brown bible. "In this text, I find a message of hope and redemption. I think you will too."

He looked out upon his flock of 10, and then out to the others beyond them. Most had paused whatever they were doing, like curious but apprehensive cats. His smiling eyes passed slowly over Delia, still and pale blue like a pool.

Then he began. "You have put me in the lowest pit, in the darkest depths. Your wrath lies heavily on me; you have overwhelmed me with all your waves. You have taken from me my closest friends and have made me repulsive to them. I am confined and cannot escape; my eyes are dim with grief."

In the pause that followed, those who were seated shifted uncomfortably. One woman standing nearby put her hands on her hips and tilted her head sideways. Delia saw her eyebrows rise like the arches of the bridge. She had to agree with what the woman was thinking: if this was a message of hope, she was a monkey's uncle.

The deep resonant voice of the minister continued. "How, you may ask, is there hope in this psalm? Why would we read about the pit of despair at the very moment we most need a better tomorrow?" He stopped and looked about, a startled expression on his face as if just now realizing the power of his words. "Because, I say to you, the darkest hour is the one before the dawn. And we must not confuse grief or despair with hopelessness. Our most wretched moments are those when we find what we are made of. We discover that the grit and determination we have needed all along reside deep within, and that the moment has come to lift ourselves up. To be better. To try harder. And to never, ever, let our plight in this world take us down. Rise up, I say! Rise up, my friends. Better days are to come!"

There was silence across the camp. A woman in a blue jogging suit who had been standing nearby listening to the words of the minister wiped her eyes. Then the minister raised up his right hand, formed the sign of the cross in blessing, and told the people to go in peace.

Delia looked at her tent and gear, drying in the sun. This, she thought, was her best source of hope and inspiration at this moment. A dry tent on a riverbank in a place where Blake would never think to look for her.

She walked over to the mayor, who was carving a piece of wood with a pocketknife while a young boy who appeared to be around eight years old looked on. The odd beauty of the moment and the rapt attention of the child kept her at bay. Fidgeting, she waited a moment before speaking. "Gerald?"

He looked up at her and smiled, a man in his element, delivering a lesson to a member of the community over which he presided. It had to be gratifying to serve these people, even if they were desperate and downtrodden.

"I was wondering," she said, stalling. "I'm new to… this." She swept a hand out, indicating the tents, the shanties, the people making food on propane stoves. "May I ask how most people here get food? Now that I'm settling in, I guess that's the next order of business."

"Well," Gerald said, rubbing a hand over the gray stubble that covered his chin. "Various ways, of course.

Some perform music. Some stand at the nearby intersections with signs and receive support from our local community. Many go to the local kitchens too… there are a few nearby. And several have jobs, you know. They work. But they're here because their wages are only enough to cover meals, necessities." He paused for a moment as if there was an item missing from the list. "Oh yes! And we have some benefactors as well, including one of our own residents."

It was at this moment that Delia noticed a man approaching the edge of the encampment. He wore a baseball cap and a red flannel shirt and had a trimmed beard. There was something vaguely familiar about him, and she wondered for a moment about past lives and premonitions.

"Ah!" Gerald said. "Speak of the devil! Michael, my friend. Good to see you!"

The man named Michael took off his baseball cap and though it wasn't much of a disguise as far as Delia could tell, cheers went up all around. Some of the small children ran to him, and he set down the shopping bags he was carrying and squatted to hug them. Delia saw a few of the women run hands over their hair, and one pressed her lips together as if she had just applied lipstick.

But in fact, Michael was hers. Or, he had been long ago. No wonder he had seemed familiar. He was the love of her high school days. Her first bright hot passion. Before she was an entrepreneur. Before she was a cook. Back when her world centered around her parents and friends, when holidays were spectacular, and she had a room of her own. Before Blake and all that came after.

Michael was distributing sandwiches and fruit. Even from where she sat contemplating the idea of disappearing into her tent, she could smell the aroma of the oranges. When he had distributed the food from the shopping bags and his backpack, and still had more to give, he looked around for anyone he had missed, and their eyes met. He began to beckon to her and then stopped.

"You," his mouth said, though she could not hear if he actually made a sound.

Then she went to him and accepted a sandwich, the idea of which made her mouth run dry, and one of the fragrant oranges, which made it water. "Are you…" she began, unable to utter the word that came after. She looked around at the camp, trying to determine if this was his home.

"It's rather a long story," he said as his eyes scanned her face. "But you won't find a person here who doesn't have a lengthy and colorful tale."

Delia nodded. His compassion was like a bread crumb trail for her to follow. She too had a colorful tale. He was acknowledging that—telling her he understood that her circumstances were likely complicated too. It put her at ease.

"Have your lunch," he said. "Then we'll talk."

She watched him as he went to talk with Gerald. Then she took her sandwich to a rocky spot near the river and found a smooth boulder where she could sit in the sun. The day was pleasant, and she watched the birds nesting and fluttering under the bridge.

From some long-ago college poetry class, Emily Dickinson's lines came unbidden, flitting into her mind like those birds.

Hope is the thing with feathers -
That perches in the soul -
And sings the tune without the words -
And never stops - at all -

"They're cliff swallows," Michael said, when he clambered down over the rocks to her. "You can tell by the flash of red you see on their heads when they flit in and out of the shadows. With barn swallows, you'll see blue."

She looked at him, studying how his face had matured and weathered. Then she began to peel the orange. "I left my husband yesterday," she said. There would likely be no better time to reveal this than the present.

"Oh. Yesterday." He seemed to be testing this idea for the weight required of truth. "So perhaps the story of how you came to be homeless does not have the long and winding path of some."

"Oh, it does." She smiled at him. "This is just the newest chapter in the shit show that is my life."

They sat for a moment watching the river flowing by. "I'm sorry for asking, but weren't there other options for you, besides a homeless encampment under a bridge? What about your mother? A friend?"

She thought of the morning, little more than 24 hours before, when Blake had slammed her against the wall, his acrid coffee breath flowing over her like the killing rasp of a dragon as he threatened what he would do to her if things were not just so when he returned from work. How she knew her mother would not believe her, because she never did. And how her best friend Marjorie would tell her to work it out. Love is too hard to find, she'd say for the millionth time. Don't give up your handsome, well-to-do husband and beautiful home. It's not worth it to be alone.

These were things one didn't explain to a perfect stranger—even one that appeared like an apparition from the past. She had needed a place where she couldn't be found. She could leave no trace.

She shook her head.

"You don't have to answer," he said. He looked out at the river and let out a deep breath. "The Reader's Digest version, for me, was that I lost my job in a corporate downsizing. No big deal, right? But I couldn't find employment after that. This was years ago. The economy was in that long downturn after 9/11. I had to give up my house and then I was sleeping on a couch at a friend's apartment. I was like on a stairway descending to hell. And one day he walked up with a bag of some blow and said, 'Let's lighten our load. Let's try this shit.' And the rest is history, as they say."

She looked at him. "And you've been living here ever since?"

"No. But I stay here regularly. I have a spot right over there." He pointed to a red tent. "It… builds trust with the community. And it keeps me humble. Meanwhile, I've recovered completely. I work and have a little house in Uptown. And I do what I can to help people here."

"That's really nice."

A small puffy cloud made its way across the sky and Delia was reminded of the soft summer afternoons of childhood. Perhaps those days weren't as bucolic and carefree as she liked to remember, but she had wanted for nothing. She had warmth and food and a bed. Her mother raised her alone, and Delia eventually got the truth out of her—about the one-night stand at her origins. It hadn't really bothered her. At least not consciously. She felt ensconced and provided for in her mother's home.

"So," she said. "You never married?"

Michael threw a rock into the flowing river. "Actually… I did. This may shock you, but I married our mutual friend, Lisa Hastings, from high school."

Delia took a deep intake of breath. "Lisa? You're kidding me."

"No, I'm afraid not."

Delia remembered that Lisa had always had the hots for him, even when she and Michael were dating. So, in one way it wasn't actually a surprise. And in fact, she couldn't have faulted Lisa for it. Delia and Michael had been together for a time, and then he had moved on. But... why had it ended? She could not recall.

She looked at him. "Well? Why did it end with Lisa?"

He shrugged. "Why does any relationship end? I was not who she thought I was. We went to a student leadership conference together senior year, and I wore a suit. What a geek! But that's what got her to sit up and take notice. Thing is, she got it all wrong. She thought I was going to climb the corporate ladder. She wanted me in Armani business suits. Rising up through increasing levels of responsibility and pay. She kept telling me I was CEO material."

He paused and watched the birds under the bridge for a while. "Evidently, she had a vision for me that I didn't have for myself. Then the economy tanked after nine-eleven and that was that. And she should see me now. A survivor of homelessness and addiction. Who knew?"

Delia watched two kids jumping and playing in the shallow water at the river's edge. Their mother stood nearby in yellow flip flops and a terrycloth sundress, smoking a cigarette.

"Hm," she said. "Misplaced expectations are at the root of most marital problems, I suspect. I seem to have traveled through a parallel universe."

He looked at her and smiled. "You wanted your husband to climb the ladder and be a big shot, huh?"

"Oh no, not at all. In fact, he was a ladder climber, but I couldn't have cared less. When I met Blake, everyone around me said I was so lucky. They told me what a catch he was. Personally, I felt more tentative. I mean, he's very successful in his private firm, but I just wanted love. Security. All that dreamy stuff some girls want. I guess I did have the lifestyle a lot of people dream of. But… it wasn't me."

She thought of the flagstone walkway leading up to her home with its professionally grown hydrangeas and box hedges. The vaulted ceilings of the great room. And beautiful mahogany furniture which was dusted weekly by their maid. And then she started to laugh.

Michael tilted his head. "What?"

"Oh my God," she said. "All we needed to do was switch partners!" After she said this, she blushed. It meant she would have been with Michael, not Blake.

"Delia. This place… it's the absolute last resort for most people. You do know there are women's shelters, right? I mean if… you're not safe."

She looked at him quickly, then away. "No," she said. "You don't understand. It's one of the first places he'd look, after my mother's house and Marjorie's — two people who would hand me over to him like a lost dog. He runs a private investigation and forensics firm. And he would find me." She swallowed to remove the tremor from her voice. "After he left for work yesterday, I walked out, dropped my cell phone and credit card in a trash can, and now I'm here. Hiding in plain sight."

Michael nodded. "I see."

He took her hand in his, and it felt just the same as it had so many years ago. A solid, warm hand that held on when you needed it to and let go when you didn't.

"There was an ice sculpture at my wedding," she said. "Two swans. Their necks entwined. I thought it meant something."

Michael let out a long, slow breath. "It certainly should have. And I bet you were a stunning bride."

She looked out at the flowing Mississippi and thought about how life is like a river. How you wade into its current and then it carries you along, and you don't know where any of it begins or ends.

When Michael stood and said he would need to take care of some business around the camp, she stood too.

"You could come by tonight if you want," she said. "There's plenty of room to sit and talk."

He nodded and said he would.

Later, they sat across from one another in her tent, her small battery-operated lantern between them. They talked about their high school days and neither of them could remember why they broke up.

"Who knows," he said. "We were young, stupid, and capricious."

Then after a moment, he stretched out on the ground next to her sleeping bag, with his hands knitted together under his head to form a pillow. And she stretched out next to him, listening to the night sounds and the hum of traffic over the bridge.

She turned to look at him. "Michael? When you were homeless, how did you… you know, stay positive? Avoid losing hope?"

"Oh, it was rough," he said. "For a while. But the human spirit is incredibly resilient. It will find its way if you give it time."

Delia nodded in the darkness, for this seemed like one true thing she could hold onto. Then she waited for more answers in the stillness that followed. But she thought that perhaps believing in possibilities was enough. She listened to Michael's calm and steady breathing and absorbed its peaceful resonance. Light from the lamp posts on the bridge filtered through the thin blue wall of her tent. She imagined it to be moonlight, lending her its magic. And the crickets hummed their familiar, reverberating summer song all around them, with a sound that was as old as time.

8

The Usher

They had brought the lights up and the people were shuffling out of the movie theater. Some were still crying. Frederick didn't really want to see that. He wasn't fond of tears. He liked the funny flicks. "Give me a comedy any day," he told Jimmy. "Why do they do that—make people cry? It seems mean-spirited."

Jimmy took one side of the theater and Frederick the other, then they split the middle section, top and bottom. Cups and spilled popcorn and all went into their bags as they moved through the rows. Frederick had a system, because if you weren't efficient, Mr. Roberts would be in there yelling at you that it's seating time for the next show. "Come on, come on. Time to open the doors."

Frederick's system was about optimizing every movement. He could have put a patent on it. He would walk down the aisle sweeping and collecting the things from the cup holders at the same time. Not just anyone could do this. It was his very own system. Jimmy could never keep up. Frederick would be done with his aisles and then he'd have to help Jimmy too. It was always like that because Jimmy was forever yammering. You can't focus if you're shooting the shit. Frederick told him that about a hundred times.

"So… my girlfriend?" Jimmy was saying. "She's having a baby."

That was the other thing about Jimmy. He always had drama. Some people just marched through life and had all the normal things happen to them, like getting their paycheck and paying the rent and so on. Not Jimmy. No, he was complicated.

This couldn't be good news, this baby. Jimmy and his girlfriend weren't married and didn't have much money. Having a kid under the circumstances was just more drama.

"Dude," Jimmy said. "Are you listening? I'm going to be a dad."

"That's great," Frederick said. "Happy for you, man. I can see you being a dad. For sure."

"Totally," Jimmy said. "It's gonna be awesome."

Jimmy was stuffing the trash into the big, wheeled trash bin and getting ready to go out the door. Frederick did a final check, because he never wanted some lady to leave her purse behind and come looking for it after people were all settled in for the next show.

This too was part of Frederick's system. On his last pass, he crouched quickly to look under each row of seats. You never knew what might get left behind. Not just purses. He found a wallet several times too. Usually, it was because guys wore those big old baggy pants that hung halfway down their butt. The perfect recipe for a wallet falling out.

He quickly looked under each row. There were no purses. Jimmy had left a cup under one of the seats, though. That was Jimmy. Not the most thorough guy. There was almost always one bag or one cup or a wadded napkin or something in the rows he said were done. As Frederick picked up the cup, he saw something else too. It was a bill, all folded up. He opened it up thinking that would be cool if it was a ten or a twenty. No one would come back for that kind of cash, and it was therefore a tip of sorts. A little thank-you from a half-thinking patron for cleaning up their mess.

This was not a ten or a twenty, however. What Frederick was holding in his hand was a hundred-dollar bill. A hundred clams. This was serious. How would the owner feel after discovering it was gone? What if it was all that person had until the next paycheck? Frederick was broke so much of the time that he could not imagine owning an extra hundred dollars all at once, let alone losing it.

He pocketed the bill. What else could he do? He would turn it in and then someone would come asking for it and he would give it back. That was the right way.

"Dude." Jimmy stuck his head back around the wall that blocked the light by the entrance. "Let's go. Why are you just hanging around in there anyway." Jimmy always asked a question like he didn't really need an answer.

They had to take their trash out back to the dumpster, and then they would usually have a quick smoke and look at the lights of the Minneapolis skyline. Frederick felt the bill in his pocket. It was like a foreign thing. He was uncomfortable with it, but the truth was he couldn't decide what to do. If he turned it in, that jerk Roberts would probably end up taking ownership. "I'll just put it in the safe," Frederick could hear him saying in his shifty way. He was the kind of guy who thought no one could see through his tactics. Smoke and mirrors. Roberts would no sooner put it in the safe than flush it down the toilet. But he'd say he was going to and then just hope everyone forgot all about it.

Frederick considered whether to get Jimmy's opinion on the matter. But no, Jimmy was too excitable.

"Dude, I can definitely help you figure out how to spend that," he'd say, bouncing on the balls of his feet.

He would have ideas about it immediately. But that didn't seem right either. A couple guys heading out to a Dinkytown bar could blow the entire wad in one night. And the whole time Jimmy would be *sharing*. That's what Frederick called it. Jimmy was the kind who was always sharing everything that was on his mind.

"She's hoping for a girl," Jimmy was saying. It was a still and balmy kind of night when mosquitoes would zing right into your ear. Even after 10 pm it felt a little hot. "Girls, though," Jimmy continued. "They're so high maintenance. So expensive. All those clothes, you know? You get a little dude, and he's all 'I don't care what I wear as long as I have me a baseball and a bat.' I prefer a boy." He was looking at Frederick as if expecting him to weigh in. As if it was just a matter of debate and once it was all settled, they could have the type of baby they wanted.

"Well now," Frederick said. "I guess it wouldn't matter to me as long as it was a healthy kid. A good kid. Not one of those noisy kids that always seems to be crying about something."

Jimmy considered this and put out his cigarette on the side of the dumpster, then chucked it in. "Dude, you are wise beyond your years," he said. "Wise beyond your years. That makes total sense." He brought out a roll of mints and popped one into his mouth and gave one to Frederick.

That was another thing about Jimmy. He was into these little extravagances.

Frederick calculated that if Jimmy bought three packs of mints per week from CVS, that was six dollars that he didn't have for groceries each week. Twenty-four dollars a month. You could buy eggs, bread, peanut butter, a bag of apples and a few frozen pizzas for that and feast on it for days. And he smoked too—an expensive, nasty habit. Frederick only smoked because Jimmy was always handing him one. He was generous that way. But Frederick, himself, hadn't bought a pack of cigarettes in a year. Not since his mother kicked him out of the house and he had to cover all his expenses with his theater income.

He thought of the bill in his pocket. He could buy a lot of groceries with that. But he didn't want to think about how to spend the money. It wasn't right. No, he'd hold onto it for safekeeping, and as soon as someone came in and asked the management for it, Frederick would pipe up and say, "Oh yes, here's your money. I found it in row nine and nearly forgot all about it." Yes, that was the way it was going to go.

But no one came to ask for the money.

That night Frederick lay in bed unable to sleep, the night a million hours long. He pictured the people who had filed out of the theater as he waited by the entrance with his broom and trash bags right before he found the bill. It was all the usual people. The groups of teen girls, the couples, the occasional loner. And Bruce, the regular guy, who walked with a limp and came to see every movie right when it came out. He remembered looking at the faces because he couldn't help it. Whenever the movie was really scary or sad, he studied the expressions of the people as they passed him by. Sometimes even the dudes were crying or looking spooked.

The thing was, he didn't remember a single guy in baggy pants. Not one. So who had dropped the C note? What he did remember, suddenly, was this one sort of swanky couple from row nine. They were not old, maybe in their twenties, but you could see they were not hurting for cash. Neat as a pin, the girl carrying what must have been a designer handbag—the type with a short handle and a little emblem on the front. Very classy. And the guy looked like a department store mannequin with groomed hair and nice duds. Even though the only thing that really registered with Frederick at the time was that they were both crying, this all came back to him now. It was like one of those dreams you have completely forgotten, and then suddenly the details come back, as if you just hadn't been looking in the right brain compartment.

He was certain now that it was this couple that lost the money in the theater. They were probably from out by Lake Minnetonka where they had lakefront property and yachts and made millions on who knows what—high tech or something—more money than he would ever have in his lifetime, even if he started saving now.

Frederick and his money were soon parted, his mother liked to say. It was one reason he couldn't live at home anymore. She said he was a bum and a couch potato, and he had to go figure things out. Plus, she had a baby with this guy she had been hanging out with for a year or so and she needed one less mouth to feed, frankly.

As he lay in bed, he thought of the hundred-dollar bill stashed away in the top of the dresser. It seemed to be calling to him, taking over his mind. He was reminded of a time as a young boy when his mother had one of her domestic moments and made chocolate chip cookies. It was such a rare occurrence that he could only remember that one time. The aroma of sweet melting buttery chocolate in the house was intoxicating. He danced around the kitchen and could think of nothing else. When the cookies came out of the oven and cooled for a bit, he was allowed to eat just one warm cookie with milk. But the magical flavor of chocolate and butter and sugar, all melded together and gooey, had drugged and bedazzled him so completely that he begged for one more. This motion was denied, and he was sent out to play.

Still, the idea of one more chocolate chip cookie consumed his thoughts, whipping him into a frenzy of desire until finally he scuttled back into the kitchen when his mother wasn't looking, pushed a chair up to the counter and reached for the container where she had stored the cooled cookies. At that moment, she entered the room, startling him, and he kicked the chair out from under himself and crashed to the ground.

This felt just like that. A kind of weird intoxication inflicted by something inanimate that should have no power over him. He believed this money was also capable of causing him far more grief and pain than whatever enticing promises it offered.

He would have to spend it. He had no choice. That is what it would take to diminish its pull on him. He would wait one more day and if no one came to the theater asking for it, he would go buy something.

Finally, mulling over the notion that he could simply spend the money and eliminate the problem of having a hundred-dollar bill tugging at his every waking thought, he relaxed at last, and fell into a fitful sleep.

When he woke again it was 5 a.m. He knew he had no more sleep left in him, and finally he rose, made coffee, and paced his basement apartment until daylight. Then he emptied the trash, swept the floors, watered the flowers and did other chores for Mr. and Mrs. Bjornson, the elderly couple who lived in the house above his basement apartment.

His mother would be proud, he thought, if she was the type of person who felt such things. Here he was doing daily chores, to offset the cost of rent, and because of that he could cover his expenses. He had never told her how he was getting on, and she never asked.

That night by the dumpster, Jimmy handed Frederick a Marlborough and gave him a questioning look. "What is it with you? It looks like somebody dropped a firecracker down your pants. Have you been snorting something or what?"

It was a legitimate question. Frederick knew he looked like he had just watched one of those horror films that practically makes your hair stand on end.

He took a drag from the cigarette. "Jimmy, do you ever have those nights where you just can't sleep? Like something's weighing on you?"

Frederick was sure he was not alone in this. Jimmy was always fretting or trying to figure something out.

But Jimmy laughed. "Nah, bro. Nothing gets between me and my sleep. You gotta get it all out of your system in the daytime."

It was ironic. Jimmy was the one always talking about his issues and concerns, and yet he somehow was the one with a clear conscience, able to sleep even with all that crazy stuff rattling around in his head.

Jimmy put out his cigarette. "So, what's chewing at you?"

Frederick thought about it. No one had come for the money. Now he believed the swanky couple from Lake

Minnetonka lost it and probably didn't even miss it. That affluent GQ guy probably just thought, "Oh well. Since I have a trust fund and all, what's a C note to me?" Something about this idea was deeply disturbing.

"Nothing, man," he said finally. "Just the meaning of life, is all."

Jimmy laughed at that too.

Frederick spent the next day in the shopping villages of Minneapolis. He traversed the city by light rail, by bus, and on foot. He stopped in the shops in the Linden Hills neighborhood, poking around boutique stores, looking for something special he might buy if he was the kind of guy who would spend money without thinking too much about it.

In one store, the focus was all decor for the Fourth of July. There were special garden flags, a patriotic mailbox cover, serving platters bedecked with stars and stripes, red and blue picnic ware, festive star-shaped deck lights, and even little cocktail umbrellas that looked like tiny round American flags. Frederick calculated that if he bought a set of patriotic picnic supplies for four, plus the picnic basket with the red, white and blue-checked picnic cloth, it would put him at ninety-six dollars plus tax. But he tried to think of three other people he could invite on a picnic and came up blank.

At 50th and France, he stopped into a men's salon and inquired about a haircut and shave. The dashing young man at the desk, who was perhaps also a fashion model, looked Frederick up and down and then smiled brightly as if to say, "Oh where are my manners?"

Out loud, he said, "And how can we help you today?" Frederick just wanted to know the cost. What if a haircut and shave cost eighty dollars and then he had to tip twenty. Bam. A hundred dollars gone in an hour. As he considered how to ask the question, the clerk rang up another spiffy-looking guy—seventy-five dollars for his styling services and another eighty-five dollars in grooming products. Frederick felt faint. He stepped out without saying anything.

The hundred-dollar bill was still in his pocket, but as he walked down Hennepin to visit the shops, he worried about being mugged so he stuffed it down in his shoe. Then he fretted that it might slip out when he wasn't looking, so he put it back in his front pocket. He walked along with his hand over it, as if it was a wily little thing. It had jumped to freedom at the movie theater. What was to stop it from doing so again?

At Urban Outfitters, he found that a nice new pair of Adidas Gazelle Super Sneakers would cost him exactly one hundred dollars. This was the best idea yet. He could use a new pair of shoes. His rundown Converse high tops were scuffed and tattered. The once-white rubber running around the edges was a grayish brown and peeling away in spots.

But he got to thinking about it as he wandered the store. If he bought new shoes, everything else he was wearing would look shabby by contrast. "You don't put lipstick on a pig," his mother liked to say, anytime a little window dressing failed at fixing the actual problem. Anyway, it was time to get to work.

On break, Jimmy didn't hand him a cigarette by the dumpster like usual. Instead, he ran a hand through his hair, fidgeted and swallowed hard. His eyes were red rimmed, as if he had been up all night studying for exams or something. Jimmy took classes at the business school. He was working on some sort of certificate or diploma.

"Dude," Jimmy said. "You gotta help me. I'm going cold turkey."

Frederick wasn't sure how he could help with this. He raised his eyebrows. Jimmy popped a mint in his mouth. "How did you do it? How did you quit your smokes? Give me your best tips. Because with this baby coming, I'm going to be a new man." He went on to say that he had been thinking about it since Marissa announced her pregnancy, and he knew what he had to do. He had smoked his last cigarette that day. He was done.

"Water," Frederick said.

"Water," Jimmy repeated. It was a question.

"Yeah," Frederick said. "Every time you want a cigarette, you drink a glass of water instead."

Jimmy looked at him skeptically. He appeared to already have the DTs. "You're the boss," he said, scraping his fingers through his hair again. "I'll try it."

Frederick felt for the bill in his pocket. No one had come for it, and he realized no one ever would. It was an evil thing. He couldn't figure out how to shake it. Jimmy was looking at him, popping more mints, scratching his cheek, not sure what to do with his hands.

Frederick patted Jimmy's shoulder. "It'll be fine. You'll be so busy drinking water and peeing. Before you know it, a week's gone by. Then you just keep going."

That night Frederick put the hundred-dollar bill in a sealed Tupperware container in the refrigerator. He put the container behind everything in the fridge—past the cold cuts and mayo, the pack of lettuce and the orange juice, as if trying to convince it of its limited importance. Then he fell into bed, exhausted, and dreamed.

In the dream he was wading in one of the nearby lakes which lay in stillness at dusk, not a duck or a gull in sight. No canoes or paddle boards or sailboats. No sound but the wind. It came in gusts, skittering across the water and ruffling his clothes and hair. Something floated past him, propelled by the breeze, a bit too far out for him to see well, and too far to reach. He stepped a little deeper into the lake. That was when a somber note sounded—a deep low cello note, like a warning.

The floating thing—a bit of paper, perhaps—seemed to wave delicately, like a flirtatious girl. He stepped deeper. The cello sound came again, longer and more ominous. Then he was floating, moving his arms through the water to reach the paper. He saw that it was a one-hundred-dollar bill.

In a moment he was well into the lake, and it was suddenly past sunset. The day's last light left the sky and the mere sliver of moon slithered behind large banks of storm clouds. The bill was in reach, at last, and as he got it into his hand, the cello music became a long low and constant drone that stilled his heart. He turned to look toward shore, but saw that it was far away now, too far for his ability as a swimmer. He held the one-hundred-dollar bill in his hand as he took his last breath of air, and felt the grip of duckweed about his ankles, tugging and pulling him into the depths.

He woke, gasped for air and sat up. He shook himself. He felt like laughing. It had been a ridiculous dream, for he was not one to go wading into lakes with night coming on. But he could not clear away the image of reaching for the bill in the water or the sight of the distant shore.

A spark of an idea came to him. This money, he realized, was only malevolent in his hands, because he had been the one to find it and had not turned it in as he should have. If Jimmy had found it, he would have taken them both out for drinks and spent it right away. Or if Frederick had turned the money in, Roberts would have been the one in its grip. It was too late for all of that, now. But what he could do was to give it away. He could give it to Jimmy and tell him to use it for the baby, or for things Marissa needed to buy. He could turn this bad thing into something good.

That entire day he rejoiced in this plan. He tidied his apartment, did his agreed-upon chores for Mr. and Mrs. Bjornson, and even mowed their lawn and trimmed their hedges, whistling and humming. Mrs. Bjornson made him iced tea and a tuna fish sandwich and set it out on the cool porch on the south side of the house. She made him sit and asked him questions. Had he met a girl? Was he in love?

Frederick just laughed. He looked at her papery hands, gripping her cane, and the silky lines of her smiling face. Mr. Bjornson sat in the living room watching a program on TV, looking contented. His life was good. You could have a good life and live into your old age and be happy, if you were a certain type of person, maybe, and had the right luck come your way. Old Bjornson lived off a nice pension. He had managed factory workers for over 40 years and saved money. Now he had no worries except what to eat for lunch.

"It's working pretty well," Jimmy said that night as they took their break out by the dumpster. He was drinking water from an extra-large Coke cup. Already Jimmy seemed less haunted and sick than he had the night before. "Quitting sucks, and I drank my weight in water today. But with that and the mints, I think I can do it."

"You can," Frederick said. He thought about how to give Jimmy the money and not make it awkward.

"I have an announcement," Jimmy said. "Something big." Frederick thought maybe he had proposed to Marissa. Jimmy would want to do the right thing. But a few moments passed, and he seemed unsure of what to say. Several other possibilities crossed Frederick's mind. Jimmy had cancer. Or Marissa lost the baby. Maybe it was something bad like that.

"I got another job," Jimmy said. "It's in management, with on-the-job training." He looked at Frederick with an awkward smile. "So, I mean, I am quitting here, of course."

Frederick couldn't think of anything to say. He and Jimmy had worked together at the theater for over two years. It wasn't like they were best friends. They didn't really hang out outside of work. Just their talks on break and the occasional beer. But how had Frederick not understood until now that Jimmy really was the closest friend he had?

"Oh," he said. "Congratulations. That's great, dude."

"Yeah, it's because I'm finishing my business degree. They hired me because of that. It's a good salary. I'll make four times what I'm making here, right off the bat."

Frederick smiled. "Good for you. It's about time one of us got a real job."

He thought of all the changes Jimmy was making in his life. Having a baby, quitting smoking, getting some corporate job, moving up, moving on. He wouldn't have the first idea how to do that. But he vowed to consider it. Maybe he had suffered from limited thinking about what was possible. He only thought about today and next week, and how to make enough money to eat.

Outside on the street after closing time, he realized the damned C note was still in his pocket. He could not bear to be with it for one more night, while it tried to steal his soul.

A few moments later, he stepped into the late-night convenience store on University Avenue to buy milk for his morning cereal, hoping there would be no issue with paying for it with a large bill. This, he was certain, would break its hold on him.

Fate had other things in store, however, and his salvation did not come from paying for milk with the hundred-dollar bill. It came from being in the wrong place at the wrong time, and was it delivered via the point of a knife.

As he entered the store, two things happened in rapid sequence. A kid standing near the counter in a ski mask and wielding a switchblade turned from the clerk to him, and the clerk did something behind the counter—pressed an alarm button or something. Frederick thought about turning to run out the door but feared being stabbed in the back. The kid's hand was shaking. Frederick could see he was just a teenager because his neck was covered in blistery red pimples.

"Move over there," the kid croaked. He needed Frederick near the clerk so he could watch them at the same time. "Both of you, give me what you've got."

Frederick reached into his pocket, which held only one item. He pulled out the folded hundred-dollar bill and held it toward the robber, steady and sure. It seemed he had never felt so calm. He could see the 100 printed on the bill, and the smug face of Ben Franklin. Unlike that night in the theater when he first found it, the 100 was right on the top. The kid looked down at it and snatched it out of his hand.

A siren could be heard, then, not far off and coming closer.

Frederick nodded his head toward the door. "You'd better run."

The kid looked at the clerk, as if to say, "I will settle up with you later, pal," then bolted out the door.

"Thanks, man," the clerk said. "Poor kid. He's all strung out. Did you see that? Just needs to know where his next hit is coming from."

The clerk was a man of about 30 or so. He had a beer gut and a little scar under his left eye. This probably wasn't his first or last robbery. He had chosen this life, or settled into it, selling scratch-offs, six packs and pucks of Skoal, and never knowing if he'd live to see another day.

Not Frederick. No. He knew in that moment he was going to aim for bigger things.

"No worries," he said. Then he laughed. "That bill was burning a hole in my pocket."

The police arrived and questioned them, but since the assailant had made off with only a hundred bucks, they really weren't going to do much. They would keep an eye out, they said.

Frederick nodded. "Just look for the pimpliest kid in Minneapolis."

Then he walked out into the night toward the lights of the city, where crickets sang in the underbrush and ducks flapped and settled down by the river. At last, he was a free man.

9

Three Things

Thing One

Happiness may not be something we decide. Ollie, for instance, does not seem to have this in his control. Every day I give him ideas about how to improve his mood. "Watch a funny show," I tell him. "Eat jellybeans. They are, by nature, hilarious." And, when that fails, "Ollie, have you noticed that Mao Mao has taken to sleeping in the potato basket?"

He looks at me, his mouth in a straight line. "It's not working, Linda. News flash. I'm not you."

I reach out to tickle him a little, but the ominous look on his face reminds me that my efforts to amuse him often make things worse.

I'm not sure when all this started. There was no beginning. I married a person who joked about everything. Dumb things. We had that in common. But *that* Ollie—the one who laughed at anything and nothing—began disappearing without me being conscious of the transition. I started losing him about five years into our marriage, like those devices you buy that seem programmed to crap out when the warranty is up.

"Honey," I tell him all the time, "it's going to be okay. You're just having a bad spell." But it's not a bad spell anymore. It's a river running through our lives.

I take the trash out on Sunday night, and I think about what a simple joy this task is. Take out the old stuff. The smelly things. Coffee grounds and used cat litter. Bacon drippings, orange rinds, and eggshells. All the things that would show a Martian about our lives.

Ollie won't take out the trash because it makes him sad. So I give him other tasks. "Honey, could you load the dishwasher? Our maid sucks, you know that? In fact, I can't remember when I last saw her."

He rolls his eyes at me. He's on the couch, watching re-runs of *Friends*. He reaches for the clicker, slowly, like it's the world's hardest task. How could he load the dishwasher if he can't even find the energy to turn off the TV?

I make a point of walking past with a laundry basket of clean, folded clothes. They are piled so high I can't see around them, so I bump into the hallway door jam on the way to the bedroom.

"Oof! Damn it."

It is my way of saying I shouldn't have to do this alone, and that perhaps depression is some kind of convenient excuse. "Just get up and help," my body language tells him. I'm never sure if I am unkind or just tired. Somewhere inside myself, I worry that the love I have for Ollie is somehow an enabler of sadness.

He will come back to me. I have to believe that. And I will be here when he's ready.

In the afternoon I finish all the cleaning. I light some candles for ambiance. It's a chilly winter day, slipping toward dusk. It is the kind of day that invites pleasures, like a fireplace, a glass of wine and some friends.

Then I tell him. "I invited the Fishers over."

He looks at me in a kind of slow alarm and gives me the wounded look of the betrayed. Company pains him. "Why didn't you tell me?"

"I *am* telling you. I'm telling you now." I tidy things up as I say this, gathering a potato chip bag and other desultory snack litter and opening a window a crack for fresh air even though Minnesota winter nights have an arctic chill that will take your breath away. Sometimes I wonder if our house smells of sadness, the way some houses smell of dog.

"Yes, but you're not *asking* me," he says from under thick eyebrows that sit above his face like rain clouds. "You don't know if this is a good day. You just think I'll come 'round."

What I don't say is that I'm well aware he will say "No" if I ask. So why would I ask? Guilt nags at me. I'm not the nicest wife these days.

He rises from the couch at last. He has no choice, which of course is the whole point. He has pig barn breath, and his hair is terrible — matted on one side from the couch pillow and sticking out like straw on the other. I shoo him toward the shower. I want the man I know he is inside, the one I married, to be whole and strong and smelling of aftershave. I think these things because the other option is panic.

When Victor and Sally Fisher come, they stomp into the front hallway like a small herd of elephants. My house smells like candles, fresh laundry, and seafood casserole.

"Come in!" Kiss kiss. "You guys look fantastic. Here, let me take your coats."

Sally rubs her arms a little bit after I take her coat, as if indoors is only marginally better than out. But she is smiling. "Dang that old Jack Frost."

Victor looks around as if wondering why I'm here doing all this greeting and coat hanging alone.

I wave my hand toward the bar. "Let's have drinks. That will take the chill off." I look toward our bedroom, where Ollie is not coming out. "Ollie's showering. He was busy with household chores, so he's running late."

It's just a small lie. It would have been true in another phase of our lives. He would have run the vacuum, made freshly cracked ice for the cocktails, cleaned the fireplace, and stacked fresh split wood in the rack. But the rack sits empty. I imagine the wood releasing its heavenly pine scent, and for a moment I feel robbed. I want to shout like some bizarre cartoon character, "Why can't I have nice things?"

Sally wants what I'm having, so I pour her a glass of cabernet. Victor says "Scotch." I hold up the Johnny Walker Red in one hand and the Cutty Sark in the other for him to choose. He taps his chin. "Eeny meeny miney mo."

Sally bumps him with her shoulder in a kind of football player move, which makes him almost fall off his bar stool. They are laughing, the way couples verging on middle-age do, when they have fallen back in love again with the kids out of the house.

"Pick one," she says. "You probably can't even tell the difference."

"Of course I can. Don't be ridiculous. Linda can test me."

Sally leans her arms on the bar counter. "Such a man. Always showing off." It's obvious that she finds it hot.

For a moment I feel envious of her. She's got a husband who shows off, and maybe even has a little chip on his shoulder. I would take it, I realize. Give me that guy — even if he can be a prick sometimes. Just not one who can't get off the couch.

And yet, I don't want someone else. I want Ollie. My wonderful, funny, lost, sad Ollie.

"I'm not showing off," Victor says. "In fact, I don't even have to taste them. I can tell by sniffing. Go ahead, Linda. Test me."

I laugh. "Okay, let's see if this man knows his scotch." I turn my back and make a big deal of moving the bottles around in front of me to mix them up.

"Abracadabra," I say for effect. We are having fun. Then I pour one finger each of Johnny Walker and Cutty in two low-ball glasses. I've almost forgotten about Ollie.

But after I take a moment to memorize which glass is Cutty and which is Johnny, and turn back around, he is standing there, a few steps into the room. He observes us from a distance, as if we are zoo animals. I almost decide to act like one—a baboon or a chimpanzee, for example— just to keep the tension from spilling into the room like a toxin.

Ollie's sudden eerie presence, in a fresh shirt that looks nevertheless a bit rumpled, is jarring. We stop laughing. Then I rush to pretend it's nothing at all.

"There you are! Come on over, darling. What will you have to drink? Scotch? Would you like that? It's what we're pouring. I can't remember whether you like Cutty Sark or Johnny Walker better."

He slowly walks the last few gallows' steps, making no eye contact. "None for me, thanks."

Victor claps him on the back. "Come on, old chap! The night is young."

That's when I see what a bad idea this is. I had hoped some company would be uplifting—a little fun to lift Ollie out of his doldrums. But it is like trying to change the direction of a current. And he's right. He really shouldn't drink. More than once he has ended up crying after a few glasses of wine.

I reach into the bar fridge for a St. Pauli, a non-alcoholic beer.

But Victor shakes his head and makes an irked little grunt. He seems personally offended that Ollie isn't drinking with us. "Don't be silly," he says to me. And then to Ollie, "It's not like you have to drive."

Victor looks at me a little sternly and I feel my happy hostess persona skidding off the road I'd mapped out.

He nods at the bottles. "He'll have a scotch with me."

I wait for the next thing, whatever it may be. Ollie shrugs. "Sure. Okay." I pour two fingers into a small glass.

Sally adjusts on her bar stool so Ollie can slide in next to her. "Wait, Linda. You didn't do the test."

"Oh yes." I put the two glasses in front of Victor. Their perfume has already released, it seems to me, along with the fun of the moment.

He sniffs one, holds it in. Releases. Sniffs the other. "This one's Cutty," he says pointing left. "This one's Johnny."

I can no longer remember which one is which. So I simply shrug and say, "You're a genius."

Soon Victor is expounding on the differences in quality and flavor of different scotch brands, explaining that Johnny Walker is superior to Cutty Sark, and how jarring it is to experience a lemon aftertaste with scotch. Sally gives him her rapt attention. I nod at certain points, barely listening. Ollie stares into his glass, sipping from time to time and trying to smile.

Victor reaches over the bar for the Black Label and tops up Ollie's drink.

"Oh hey," he says. "I've got a great joke for you guys. Goes like this. Two jumper cables walk into a bar. One of them says, 'We'd like a couple of beers, please.' And the bartender says, 'Okay, but don't start anything!'"

Sally guffaws. I pound the bar with the flat of my hand. "I bet you've got a million of them."

"Of course!" Victor is already well into his refill of scotch now, and his eyes are looking glassy. "This one will knock your socks off. Okay, so why did the woman bring a ladder to the bar?"

Sally and I shake our heads. Ollie slugs back the rest of his drink.

Victor looks at each of us. "Anyone? No? It was because she heard the drinks were *on the house*! Get it? Like on *top* of the house?"

Sally and I smile at each other and shake our heads. The cabernet is smooth and has been going down readily enough. Suddenly, laughing seems like something you might do on another plane of existence, or in a galaxy far far away, where no one's sadness fills the space like helium. And I wonder for a moment if anyone is ever truly happy.

Just then, Ollie rises. He addresses a place on the wall where there is bland paint and nothingness. "I'm sorry. I really haven't felt well all day." He nods to Sally but ignores Victor. Then he walks off to the bedroom and is gone.

The Fishers look at me. I feel heat tinge my cheeks. I grope for something to say and can only manage, "Sorry about that."

Victor releases an angry snort. "What's up with him?"

"Ollie is just… out of sorts." I'm torn at that moment between keeping Ollie's secret and telling them everything. I want to say, "Ollie is depressed out of his gourd. I don't know what to do. I'm so sad for him. And so very very scared." Instead, I try to think of a way to fill the glum silence.

Sally swirls the remaining red wine in her glass. "Maybe he needs some help. Has he seen anyone?"

Has he *seen* anyone? Ah, there it is. The universal phrase insinuating that someone with an official title can fix this, the same way a surgeon fixes a blocked artery. They wait for an answer. Because if I say Ollie *hasn't* seen anyone, it would be like complaining of a headache and not taking a pain killer. Which means the only answer is one that infringes upon Ollie's privacy.

"Yes, he has, actually. For quite some time." I think of Doctor Hansen. The perfect doctor. I think of all the things we've tried. The therapy sessions. The pills. The ones that did nothing, and the ones that made things worse. And my fear that Ollie is truly broken and can't be fixed.

Victor laughs. "Ha! Well, the old boy needs to buck up. Does he think he's the only one who has been dealt a bad hand? Does he know how many people have it worse off than he does?"

Sally covers Victor's hand with her own. "Hush, Vic. He'll hear you."

"That's alright!" Victor suddenly speaks in a drill sergeant voice. "He should! He needs a good swift kick, is what he needs!"

I stare at him, unsure of what to do or say. But Sally sits up straight. "Victor, I'm telling you to stop."

"Well just look." Victor gestures at me and then around the room. "The man's got this beautiful home, and a lovely, hard-working wife. Maybe he should visit Ethiopia. Or Bangladesh. Get an idea of just how privileged he really is."

I feel my heart pounding in my neck, arteries preparing to burst. I have only one sentence in me. So I choose this one. "Ollie doesn't want more than he has."

Somehow, even though it isn't an answer, this statement brings the conversation to a close. They push their glasses across the bar. Sally smiles and Victor gets up and stretches. "Well," he says. "Some other time, maybe."

The aroma of my seafood casserole wafts from the kitchen. I help them retrieve their coats. We kiss goodbye. And I wonder if it is possible to live a normal life.

Thing Two

There isn't always a reason for things that are off kilter. Out of balance. We want to point to causes. But there isn't always a cause—at least not one we understand. You hear all the time about some kid who was nice to everyone, if a little reserved, and therefore no one ever imagined he was building bombs in the basement.

It is Monday evening, the night when men everywhere are watching football, eating chips and making manly sounds. Ollie is sitting on the floor in the living room in his underwear, staring silently at the wall.

I sit in the overstuffed chair near the coffee table, cracking walnuts. It is one of the things I do to make things normal. *We're just here enjoying some together time and eating nuts.* From time to time, he looks at my hands, at the nutcracker, as if they are alien things, or a personal affront to his sensibilities.

I ask Ollie what makes him sad, and he says there is nothing. Then he says it's not any one thing. And finally, in an aggravated tone, he says, "Why does there have to be a reason? It just *is*."

"Because," I tell him. "If we knew the cause we could try fixing it. If I told you the car kept coughing and giving up at the side of the road, you would want to investigate it, right? Then you could try to fix the conditions that cause this problem. Everything would be better."

He stares at me for a long minute. I realize I've compared his depression to a sputtering car. Like he just has some mechanical problem. I put my hand over my mouth and shake my head. "I'm sorry. It was a bad analogy, wasn't it? I take that back. It was only…. Well, it was a metaphor. An illustration that you can't fix anything that you don't know the cause of." I'm talking too much.

Ollie points to my hand. "Look at that walnut you're holding."

I look down at it. Like all walnuts, it is wrinkled, hard and brown. But it is a thing of beauty. A weird small alien thing that nature made. And inside is something we call *meat*, even though it is the nut itself. It is a crunchy bit of wonderfulness. It is the true essence of what we mean when we say the word *nut*.

Ollie seems to search for words. He wants to tell me something that will help me understand. But he looks down, shakes his head.

"What? What is it about the walnut, honey?"

He sighs, evidently exhausted by this exercise. But he tries anyway. "When you look at the walnut you see... I don't know, food? I look at it, and it seems to me to be the saddest thing I have ever seen. I feel like the walnut is making me depressed. Do you see?"

I want to see. I want to understand. But I shake my head. "A walnut, Ollie?"

"Yes. But I mean, no. It is also the shower curtain. The shower curtain is so terribly sad. I can touch the shower curtain with my hand, and sadness comes off of it like rain."

I think of my bright shower curtain, with its turquoise blue waters like the sea of Cozumel, and its brilliant yellow and red fishes, all swimming with purpose. I look at him. "Those two things? The walnut and the shower curtain?"

"And my pants. I could not put on my pants today. They were too sad. And the newspaper, with its smell of news and paper and ink, of politics and murders and global warming."

He grimaces. Then he goes on. "Also that child next door, who is sent out each afternoon to clean up the dog poop in the yard. He bends down to pick it up from the snow. With a scoop. I can't breathe when I see that, Linda. It strangles me, and I have to look away. Plus. There is that crack in the driveway. Whenever the snow melts it is revealed again, like some scar. Like decay." After he says this, his shoulders droop and he looks down at his hands. He is utterly exhausted from the effort.

Now I think I understand. It is all of those things, and it is nothing. There is no cause, but everything is a cause. I can't feel what Ollie feels, any more than you can feel another person's pain if they are cut with a knife, burned or bludgeoned. I can only listen and hope my constant presence and my love for him will somehow, someday, make it better.

All I can say then is, "I will make us some tea."

In the kitchen, I put the kettle on the stove and breathe. Tears I have never cried roll down my cheeks and I wonder if I can keep doing this. And then the water boils and I summon more patience and more love than I have ever needed for anything in my life. More than is required for the sassy and annoying eighth graders I teach.

"Ollie. My sweet Ollie. You will be well again. It is only a matter of time." I make that my new mantra.

It seems to me it started when his mother died, but that makes no sense. She was an angry, god-awful woman that made everyone around her feel like shit. She criticized me and my housekeeping, made fun of obese people and anyone underprivileged, threatened small children on the sidewalk if they didn't move aside. I try not to think about the mix of guilt and relief I felt when she had a sudden, massive stroke and was gone. It made me feel uncharitable and unkind. I cross myself as if I believe in God unequivocally and want to make sure I don't go to hell.

Ollie has told me of the childhood he endured. How his mother scolded him for any misdeed, no matter how small, and ridiculed him for any grade but an A. How she slapped him if he said *darn*, or any other word that could somehow be interpreted as a cuss word. As an only child, he bore the brunt of her tirades, and his father was too afraid of her to intervene. When I met him, he seemed unphased by it all, as if he had kicked all of the memories to the curb and moved on. But maybe the troubles of the past never leave us. Perhaps, like an untended garden, our abandoned memories slowly become strangling weeds and take over everything that may have tried to flower.

When I return to the living room with a tray, Ollie is gone.

"Ollie?"

I set the tray down on the coffee table and begin walking through the house. He is not in the spare room, or in our bedroom. At last, I find him in the den. He is looking at our wedding photo, still dressed only in a t-shirt and underwear.

For a moment I feel hopeful. This effort of his to come to this room, to open this book, seems like a step in the right direction. It's something any normal person would do.

As I watch from the doorway, he looks up at me, his eyes gray and deadened from pain. "Who was I then?" he asks me, holding up the photo like an offering, like a sacrificial lamb. "What happened to that guy?"

Thing Three

Perhaps at the heart of all devastation is what is gone from us. Or what we cannot find. Ollie's happiness is like a possession unaccountably lost — like a certain book or a family photo that got devoured by time or lent out and never returned.

One day I return from work and cannot find Ollie anywhere. I look from room to room, thinking he must have gone off somewhere. But he never goes out anymore.

It occurs to me that he should consider taking a job again, even though his inheritance makes it unnecessary. Having to report into an office might be good for him. And I would fret about him less.

"Ollie? Honey, where are you?"

There is no answer. Every room is empty. Panic grips me as I check closets, bathtubs, the basement.

At last, I see a light in the workshop behind the house, and I dash out across the snow. I squeak the door open. He is there, putting things in boxes.

"Hey buddy. What's up?"

He packs away some woodworking tools, a blow torch, and a small burner he used to use to heat wax to make candles. "I don't need this stuff."

"Why not? Maybe a hobby project would do you some good."

Even as I say this, I know it's futile. Ollie tried so many things. Model cars, stamp collecting, candles, and even beer making. He seemed to be searching for just the right project that would help him find the essence of himself. But one day, when a batch of beer exploded, he quit everything. He cleaned up the beer mess, and then closed the door on the workshop. As far as I know, he has not been out here since. Was that it? Was that when it all started?

He sets a tin of wood stain in the box. "What is the point of it? It is like keeping the ruins of a house after it burns down in a fire."

"Maybe you should work on something—you know, just for relaxation. For the fun of it. Kind of in a Zen way. Not to be an *artiste* or make something great."

"Don't be dumb, Linda. All these things remind me of ideas that have come and gone. I left them here like Hansel and Gretel's breadcrumbs, hoping they would lead me back to something. But they never did."

I repeat my inner mantra that Ollie will be well again. It is only a matter of time. But there is no wellness to be found here in this cold old shop with all of these memories of things he has tried and abandoned.

"Tell you what," I tell him. "Sleep on it for a night. Let's go see a movie, come home, get a good night's rest. Then tomorrow I'll help you get all this done."

Ollie looks around the room, at the ghosts of his projects, and nods. Dealing with this would be daunting for a well person. But for someone who is overwhelmed by the task of getting out of bed each morning, it must be crushing.

We head downtown. The moon is out, lovely and full, and the air is crisp. I remember times, early in our marriage, when we went ice skating at Centennial Lakes in winter. I remember that feeling of bliss, our breath coming out in puffs, and the sense that all the wonderful things lay in wait, ready for us to discover them. The theaters, the shops, the Dinkytown restaurants and downtown bars. We could go to the ice sculpture festival. In the summertime, we could do a paddleboat cruise on the Mississippi. I yearn for the things we have not done.

At the theater, we get tickets for a comedy called "Hail, Caesar," in which George Clooney plays a movie star. "Art imitates life," Ollie says. The movie is more charming than funny. It's one of those flicks where the star power eye candy is more worthwhile than the substance. Scarlett Johansson, for example, takes my breath away.

We emerge from the theater, and the magic of the film's ambiance dissipates like fog. We walk along the street, looking out at St. Anthony Falls, the Stone Arch Bridge and the city skyline. I steer Ollie uptown toward University Avenue and the light rail. I want us to get on and ride, to see the city lights, to have everything open up for us again like a tree surrounded by gifts at Christmas.

"Poor Clooney," Ollie says.

"What do you mean?"

"He's so… old. So washed up." Ollie is walking slowly, as if each step pains him, like a stiff old man.

"I thought he looked pretty good." Even though I say this, I have to admit that he seemed sort of gray and withered. In the movie, he was kidnapped and held ransom, which painted him as such a weak, two-dimensional character that I found myself losing interest. I worry I am slipping into Ollie's world.

Ollie sighs from deep within himself. "He is just like that walnut. Wrinkled and sad."

"Or the shower curtain."

Ollie stops. He closes his eyes. He is breathing so shallowly that it seems he might just sleep here, standing up. "Why are we here?"

I'm not sure how to answer. The temperature is dropping. I want to get on the train and become enveloped in its warmth. "I thought we might ride. You know? Just see some city lights. Enjoy the warmth of the train and looking out the window at the snowy landscape."

Ollie looks down the tracks and I send him silent signals to find joy in this. To enjoy the expectation, just like a child, that soon the train will come. We will get on that train, and we will ride.

But that is not what happens. The train comes into view, and we watch it glimmering on the tracks, its lights coming steadily toward us. But in a tiny, crystalline fragment of time that slows down just briefly before speeding up again, I realize something so mortifying that I cannot breathe. Ollie is doing math. He is calculating distance and time.

I grip his arm. "Ollie."

He looks at me. The pain I see in his eyes is so excruciating that I cry out.

He peels my fingers from his arm. "Linda. My wonderful wife. I am... so sorry." He carefully releases the last finger—my left pinky. And then he leaps.

A Fourth Thing

They say that in moments of extreme stress people can exhibit superhuman strength—an adrenaline-charged superpower they would never possess in normal life. People have lifted cars and tractors off loved ones and have fought bears with nothing but their hands to protect their children. This phenomenon even has a name: *hysterical strength*.

And I know why it happens. In an extreme circumstance, the body overcomes the limitations of the mind. For just a brief moment, it does the thinking. It makes the decision to act, without the mind to tell it what it is or is not capable of. I know this to be true, because when Ollie peels my last finger from his arm, for a nanosecond my mind believes I have to let him go. That it is better for him to experience one horrible, bright hot moment of extreme pain than to be under the crushing weight of depression for one more day.

But my body says no. No! And even as Ollie leaps, I lunge harder, faster, with an adrenaline-fueled aim that my mind has no time to contemplate. With hysterical strength, I grab his arm, and I pluck him from his flight, yanking him toward me so hard that both of us spill backwards, crashing onto the platform. Excruciating pain stabs me upon landing as my back and then skull slam into a concrete bench. And the people around us scream.

Epilogue

Ollie and I are wheeled away from each other to separate wards to recover from the head and spine injuries sustained in our backward fall. My bed is in a regular hospital unit, for regular people with regular health problems. Ollie is under watch in a healthcare unit equipped with psychiatrists. He will be supervised. He will undergo treatment for those who have attempted, or are at severe risk of attempting, to commit suicide. He will be cared for and will be given tools for living life again. A new doctor will have him try yet another medication, under supervision, and it will show signs of being promising. I feel certain of this at the very fiber of my being.

For the first time in many months, I find myself sleeping for long periods. Sometimes I wake up shaking, hyperventilating, trying to find a better way to tell Ollie that he is needed, and he is loved. But then the nurse gives me something. And again, I sleep.

It will be weeks before I get to be with Ollie, to hold his hand, and walk with him. Meanwhile, I find time to ponder. To think about this man. My husband. About every sweet thing about him that is still in there somewhere. I know now what he was looking for and could not find. It is the thing I have never lost, but that for some people goes tragically dormant. It is hope for tomorrow, and the belief that something good is in store.

Beyond this moment, I believe, is something even better. There are trains to ride and museums to visit. There are children laughing in the snow in winter, and in summer they are waving sparklers. I want to throw my hat in the air on a street corner like Mary Tyler Moore. I want to walk across the Stone Arch Bridge by moonlight, see a concert in the bandshell with friends at Lake Harriett on a summer night. Fall in love all over again. Have a baby. Get a puppy. Live life and grow old.

I want to package this feeling into a gift for Ollie—for my own Ollie, and for *every* Ollie who is uncertain whether tomorrow is worth living for. Here it is, my love. I give you this. A seed of light and hope.

10

The Lake Home

"**L**ook, look!" Alexandra was pointing out across the lake where a boat had capsized near the channel.

Forest stepped out onto the veranda with his cocktail. He saw that the crew on board all appeared to have life jackets, so that was something.

"Idiots," he said. "Every year somebody navigates that channel drunk or brainless, scrapes on those rocks, and down they go."

"The Coast Guard is coming."

Indeed, they were. Forest could see the Guard boat and two police boats scurrying across Lake Minnetonka, lights flashing. Other yachts and small pleasure craft were gathering around the scene as well. He shook the ice in the bottom of his drink. "It's always good for entertainment, anyway."

Alexandra sighed and picked up Rexy, her Pekinese. "I know. Otherwise, I'd die of boredom here. That's a fact."

"Oh Alex. Are you serious?" he asked. "There's so much here. It's paradise."

He tried not to sound on edge, but she was exasperating. These were the first days of summer. The season of fishing, reading the news on a deck chair, and taking the boat out for a spin. Not to mention cocktails under an evening sun, and enjoying this view. All the good things. How could one be bored?

In the painful silence that followed, he offered up one of his favorite old adages. "Plutarch said that the mind is a fire to be kindled."

"Oh, don't Plutarch me, Forest. Honestly."

They looked upon the drama out by the channel, where two women, two men, a white Labrador retriever, and a beer cooler were being rescued from the sinking vessel.

Alexandra turned to him. "Anyway, when my sister and her husband visit this evening, could you please be on your best behavior? By that I mean, no proselytizing. And no tiresome monologues."

Forest gave her a solemn bow. He really did have good intentions. She would see that if she wasn't so touchy. "You have my word."

The lake home had been his idea. An extended honeymoon get-away. They had married the moment his divorce was final and then what he really wanted was a fresh start, away from the suburbs and sprawl. Alexandra, however, was a town girl. Her girlfriends, her book club, and her dog-walking pals all lived in the quaint little villages of Minneapolis, near parks and shops. They gathered weekly, drawn inexorably to one another as if chattering over iced teas at an eatery in Edina, and orchestrating puppy play dates were fuel for the soul.

Truthfully, something had nagged at him when he finally won the battle and she agreed to move out here to the lake. Yet he convinced her this lifestyle would be good for her. He talked of the parties they would have and the friends they would make—like the salesperson he was—and it clinched the deal. But here they were, two years into the lake life, and he had to admit it wasn't going well. Only a 30-minute drive from her friends, Alexandra seemed to be losing touch with them. On-the-fly get-togethers happened that she couldn't join. She was withering like a flower needing water.

The arrival of Alexandra's sister Pat and her husband Rob was just as expected. They bustled in the door, bearing a box of donuts (there was always an awkward hostess gift of some kind), whereupon they kissed Alex's cheek and shook Forest's hand before eyeing the drink cabinet.

Determined to make this work, Forest accepted the box of donuts, nodding appreciatively with eyebrows aloft before setting the carton on an end table and hoping they couldn't see through his charade. Donuts, for god sake!

"What can I pour you? We can take a cocktail out to the veranda." Even as he said this, he knew it sounded stuffy. Pretentious. His in-laws simply brought it out in him. There was no other explanation.

"Oh, just a little scotch and soda for me," Pat said, patting her stomach as if she was being offered a meal. "Rob, honey?"

Forest would have started mixing Rob's Manhattan right away, as his choice never varied, but the game was that Rob liked to pretend to think about it. And Forest, therefore, liked to make him wait. Sometimes he would act as if he didn't have Manhattan ingredients on hand. He'd search and rattle in the bar cabinets, and pop back up to ask if there was something else Rob might have in mind before snapping his fingers and remembering where he kept some backup supplies. He fancied that he could see beads of sweat gathering on Rob's forehead as the anticipation grew to a crescendo.

"Hmm," Rob said on this particular evening. "What's good today, Forest?"

This was when Forest busied himself polishing glassware that had invisible spots.

Rob and Pat Parker were from Hopkins, a small, no-consequence town where houses were the size of Forest and Alexandra's veranda. Even so, it was clear they had trouble making ends meet. Rob sold Persian rugs, and Forest suspected he wasn't very good at it. Pat taught 7th-grade physical education at Hopkins Middle School. She was a coarse, boxy woman. For that reason alone, Forest would never have picked her from a line-up as a blood relation to Alex, who was lithe and walked on air. Plus, they just seemed to have been raised on two different sides of the tracks.

Finally, Forest said to Rob, "Want a scotch and soda, like your lovely bride?" He knew he could have had the desired Manhattan in Rob's hand by now, but he felt a little of the devil in him. He could sense Alex giving him the look.

Rob put a finger to his chin and appeared to contemplate. "Actually, how about a Manhattan?"

"One Manhattan, coming right up!" Forest began pulling out the bourbon, vermouth, and bitters. "Say, did you know this cocktail originated at the Manhattan Club in New York City? I'm sure I hardly seem like the cocktail historian, but I've become interested of late."

He poked a cherry with a tiny sword and set it in the drink so that it nestled against the glass, balanced on ice, a favorite touch of his. Then he waited, holding it in his hand, knowing how badly Rob wished for it to be transferred to his. "Yup. It's been around since the late nineteenth century. Can you believe it?"

"Huh," Rob said, eyeing his drink.

"Shocking, I know. You'd think it was invented in the forties or something, wouldn't you?" Finally, in a gesture of mercy, he extended the Manhattan in Rob's direction and let him take it.

Pat nodded and looked thoughtful, but her attention seemed focused on something else, like someone who was planning a chess move.

"Yes," Forest continued. "In fact, there are records of it in various texts in the eighteen-nineties timeframe…"

"Come on," Alex said. "Let's all go out to the deck." She glanced at Forest. "We'll talk about something that interests everyone."

He noted the word *veranda* had vacated her lexicon.

They stepped out into the pleasant evening and sat in the patio chairs. The setting sun glowed with an almost holy aura. Forest felt just a touch uncomfortable at times like these, as if the splendor of this home and this view should be tempered with modesty. He wouldn't want any hard feelings. No unspoken questions like, "why you, not us?"

"This is gorgeous," Pat said. "Such a spectacular view!"

"It's grand," Rob said. "Absolutely grand."

"Some imbeciles capsized a boat out there a few hours ago," Forest said, pointing toward the channel. He was pretty certain this was a safe subject, since Alex had been so excited about it. "You have never seen such incompetence as the brilliant display we were witness to today."

Rob and Pat sat up and looked out over the water as if the event might still be happening now.

"Okay," Alex said. "Let's have a toast, shall we? To family, to gatherings, to… companionship and conversation." She raised her glass, and the other three followed suit, holding their glasses out toward each other and air-clinking them before proceeding to drink.

Forest thought of weddings and momentous occasions. Births and deaths. Things that were truly worth ruminating over and toasting. He wasn't absolutely sure what this was.

Alex shifted in her chair. She was always a nervous hostess. "So… what shall we talk about? Not politics! Definitely. Sore subject around here. Ha ha." She nodded toward Forest.

He couldn't think what she was suggesting. Certainly, the current clown in the White House wasn't to his taste.

Had she actually been listening to his mutterings over the news?

Rob scratched his chin. "Actually, we did have something to talk with you about." He looked over at Pat, who had Rexy on her lap and was cooing to him, in between sips of her scotch and soda. She seemed completely unaware that Rob had just handed her an invisible baton.

After a moment, Rob said, "Pat?"

Rexy had rolled over to his back so she could pet his tummy and she obliged. "Isn't he just the sweetest?"

"Pat." Rob set his drink down on the glass top of the end table with such a decisive clack that she had no choice but to look up at him.

"Yes. Right." She cleared her throat in the manner of one recovering from a messy chest cold. "So here's the thing. For us, I mean. With the Persian rug market taking a bit of a downturn and all?" She looked at them expectantly, almost as if she were asking a question that needed answering, before she continued. "The store where Rob works has, unfortunately, had to furlough him, is what's happened."

Rob nodded and scratched behind an ear, which, like its counterpart on the other side, had turned scarlet. "True enough."

Alex leaned forward. "Oh no. That's terrible."

Pat looked down at Rexy as if she might get some help with what she had to say next. "Which means, we really just cannot make it. Not on my teacher's salary. No way."

Rob agreed. "Nope. No way."

Pat smiled at Forest reassuringly, which did nothing to abate the rising sensation of alarm he encountered at that moment.

"So," she said, "we thought, if we could just stay with you two for a bit until Rob is employed again, it would really help."

"And you have extra rooms here," Rob added brightly, sweeping a hand toward the house. "There's quite a lot of space."

Forest sat up. Somehow, getting acquainted with Rob these past few years and having dire suspicions about his ability to fully support himself, he had neglected to conjure up this possibility in his imagination. "Well… we could certainly give it consideration."

But Alex clapped her hands together. "No, no, we don't need time to consider. You know we'd love to have you! When can you move in?" She followed this with a look that dared Forest to utter one word to the contrary.

"Yes," he said, now feeling a cold dread sliding down his scalp. "That's what I intended to say. I was just… a little caught off-guard. You'd be welcome in our home."

Pat set Rexy down and stood up as if she meant to go pack her bags immediately. "I'll call the boys," she said.

Then she added, "Oh!" But she seemed tongue-tied and did not elaborate further.

Rob rescued her by filling the void. "There's just one catch."

Forest tried not to roll his eyes. Evidently the fabulous prize of having two people invade their home was hampered by a catch of some sort.

"The boys are just headed home from college up at North Dakota State. We hope it won't be too much trouble for them to stay too. Just for the summer, of course."

Forest smiled at Alex. "Oh goody."

Forest and Alex had married too late to have children, and she adored her nephews. Objections would be futile.

"It will be wonderful," Alex said. "They're such good boys. They can take the boat out. What a great summer we'll have!"

Forest slumped in his chair. "I guess it's settled then."

◆ ◆ ◆

The nephews were named Shawn and Liam, which Forest found amusing, since neither Rob nor Pat had a smidgen of Irish blood, as far as he knew. The move-in happened just two days after the dreaded cocktail night, but he had never seen Alex so excited. In preparation, she bought new sheets for the guest rooms and even decorated the boys' room with NDSU paraphernalia. Forest dutifully installed a TV in their bedroom and also hired an electronics store to set up a home theater in the basement. Just before their arrival, he tossed back a quick martini to calm his nerves and immediately felt more gracious.

Alex was waiting by the door like an overly enthusiastic spaniel. More so even than Rexy, who had a habit of doing hyperactive spins when anyone visited. The new arrivals were only partway up the steps when Alex threw the door open. "Hello! Welcome!"

Forest was certain he had never experienced such chaos. The bags and duffels and satchels that came through the door made the foyer look like a refugee camp.

Alex kissed everyone on the cheek before issuing directions. "Pat, I'll show you and Rob to your room, and Forest here will take the boys. Rexy, you stay out from underfoot, now!"

Forest just smiled at the boys and pointed the way down the hall to the wing off the kitchen.

They dutifully followed him, while he asked them questions about what they were studying (one biology, the other something else that also ended in ology, which he had never heard of) and attempted to assess how he was going to remember which was which. They were fraternal twins and had nothing more than their dark brown hair color in common. So it should have been easy. And yet, anytime there was a fifty-fifty chance of guessing correctly, Forest knew he would only be right half the time.

Finally, since Liam was taller and thinner, and Shawn shorter and stockier, he quietly chose the monikers of Lean Liam and Short Shawn.

"So," he said, "you boys like to go boating? Fishing? Water skiing?"

They were standing in the boys' room, where they had each chosen a bed and had begun setting down their bags and duffels. Shawn and Liam looked at one another.

"We're more the gaming types," Shawn said.

"Ah. What sort of games? Chess? Backgammon? That sort of thing?"

The boys laughed. They thought he was kidding.

"No," Liam said. "Video games. But don't mention board games or parlor games to our parents. They are FA-NAT-ICS."

"Duly noted! Well. Anytime you want to explore the lake a bit, you just let me know." There was a lengthy pause during which it became clear they would be more comfortable with him gone. "Okay boys, settle on in. I'll see you at dinner."

"Thank you," they said in unison before turning away to unpack.

♦ ♦ ♦

Dinner was an elaborate affair involving a large falling-off-the-bone roast and a mountain of buttery herb potatoes. Alexandra had outdone herself. There was even fresh homemade bread and a small plated savory salad at each place—bibb lettuce dotted with pomegranate seeds and drizzled with homemade lemon vinaigrette. She knew how to impress. And Forest found her beautiful, with her hair softly wispy from steam and her cheeks tinged pink. When no one was looking, he kissed her neck. And when she smiled at him, he was surprised at the odd realization that he missed her, though he saw her every single day.

Dinner went as well as could be expected. Forest observed that Rob and the boys were all about the meat.

"Oh my God, this is like a little bit of heaven right here," Rob said. He had tucked a napkin into the V of his plaid button-down shirt like in old movies.

Forest tried not to notice how noisily this family ate—with loud chewing sounds, cutlery clanking on plates, and audible slurping when they drank. He'd had the pleasure of peace for so long that it was jarring, like hearing someone sing off-key.

Short Shawn drank a big gulp from his milk glass. "Mom, you've got to get this recipe from Alexandra."

Alex smiled, clearly pleased. "Well, of course."

"You don't seem like sisters," Lean Liam said in the blunt manner of the youthful. He glanced back and forth between his mother and Alexandra.

Pat laughed. "People have been saying that for years, but you should have seen us when we were young. We looked much more alike back then."

Forest tried to imagine this.

"And we were absolutely inseparable," Alex said. "Two peas in a pod."

Pat said, "Patricia and Alexandra!"

And Alex said, "We thought we were princesses."

Pat shook her head. "Ha. Only for a while. Then I became a tomboy."

"You did! And I could never keep up with you after that."

Forest watched this historic analysis transpire and mused how two completely different branches could grow from one tree. He had been an only child, himself, so the whole sibling thing was a mystery.

"How about you, Rob? I don't think I've ever heard you talk about your home life."

In fact, Rob never talked about himself at all. He'd never spoken of his job, or what he'd studied in school. Alexandra had mentioned that he had done some other work before the rug store, but she also admitted to knowing few details. "Did you have brothers? Sisters? Traditional family and all that?"

Rob's look was inscrutable. There was just a whisper of something secretive and bleak that crossed his face. "Ah, no. Actually, it was just me and my mom. No siblings. And my dad wasn't really in the picture, like at all." Then, in the manner of a turtle returning to its shell, he picked a slice of bread from the basket and began dabbing at a small pool of gravy on his plate.

"At least you had your mom all to yourself then, hm? Every boy's dream, am I right?"

Forest winced at a sharp kick to his shin under the table, and then noticed the dead-level stare of Alexandra. Were there landmines absolutely everywhere? She gave the slightest shake of her head as if a bruised shin was not a clear enough message.

Pat began gathering plates at that point, and Alex joined her in clearing the table. Forest stood up. "No ladies, let me clean up here. It's only fair." He had a sudden fear that Rob would offer to dry or put away.

But Alexandra was not done being the unambiguously gracious host. "I'll help Forest," she said to Pat. "You guys go start a game or something. There's a whole selection in the family room. We'll join you as soon as we're done."

Rob removed the napkin from his shirt. "Are you sure? We don't want to be freeloaders or anything."

Forest scoffed, then pretended he had just needed to clear his throat.

"Yes, my dears," Alex said. "We want to make sure your first night here is just perfect. And you must be exhausted!"

Pat made a shooing motion to Rob and the boys. "Alright then, if you insist. Guys, let's play charades. I'm so excited!"

When they could be heard assigning teams and discussing game rules in the family room, Forest said, "What was that all about?"

"You need to read the room, Forest."

"Honey, what was I supposed to read? I know I can be a lunk-head but tell me what signs I missed."

She reached to take the rinsed plate from him and place it in the dishwasher. "You just have to be more intuitive. Rob was really uncomfortable. Didn't you see that twitch in his left eye?"

"I thought it was the right eye."

"No matter. Just... don't be so nosy. No more Spanish Inquisitions. I want them to be comfortable here."

Forest handed her another plate. "Scout's honor." He tried to imagine what must have befallen old Rob in his tender youth. Perhaps his mother was one of those Mommy Dearest types.

After the dishes, they joined the others in the living room, where the first game of charades was winding down.

"Oh, too bad we missed it," Forest said.

Pat had the happy glow one sees on the faces of winners on The Price is Right. "We can play again, now that you're here!"

The boys seemed to be sulking. Lean Liam said, "Is there anything else to do? Mom always wins."

Alex informed them of the XBox in the downstairs game room and the boys excused themselves and raced off, thundering down the stairs like a small herd of wildebeests.

Before Pat could suggest another game, Forest offered drinks. "I'm feeling like a stiff one myself. What about you folks?"

"Hm, I just might join you," Rob said. "What are you making?"

To keep the peace, Forest said, "Manhattans." Then he glanced at Alex who smiled. At last, he had wizened up and had done what was expected of him. "Ladies?"

"Chardonnay," they said, nearly in unison, and then they laughed, and it occurred to Forest again that perhaps it had been a mistake to bring Alex out here, away from her friends and the epicenter of activity.

When they had their glasses of wine, Alex said to Pat, "Come on, Sis, you've got to see the moon coming up on the water. But bring a sweater because it's chilly at night."

"I'll be fine," Pat said. "I'd be hot in a snowstorm."

Alex turned to look at Forest and Rob as she and Pat walked toward the veranda. "You boys going to be alright?" She said this with the implacable warning glance that Forest had become intimately familiar with since the Parker family arrived.

He wanted to plead not to be left alone with Rob. Instead, he nodded and said, "Of course." Then the room went quiet with the women gone, and he felt a little lost and couldn't look at Rob at all.

For a moment, they remained standing in their spots by the bar with their Manhattans, as if they were actors frozen on a stage waiting for the lights to come up. Forest had lost his script.

Rob stared at the large landscape painting on the wall over the piano. "This isn't what you think," he said, cradling his glass.

"Oh?"

"No, not at all.

Forest shifted uncomfortably. It seemed too late to ask Rob if he wanted to sit down, so he leaned against the bar. "What are we talking about exactly?"

"Us. Being here. I mean, I appreciate your gracious hospitality. But we won't be needing it for long. That's all."

Forest nodded. For a moment he tried to imagine what it must feel like to ask someone to take your family in. Certainly, it would be humbling. Unless, of course, you were just that type, and were used to asking for handouts, favors, that sort of thing. "So," he ventured, "you'll be going back to work, then? Back to… the rug store?"

Rob stared at him. "No. To my profession. I've just received a job offer."

Several ways of asking what this profession might be came to mind, and Forest rejected all of them as patronizing. *You have an actual profession? What could be more exciting than rug sales?* He could hear the women talking and laughing out on the veranda, and the boys whooping over something entertaining in the basement. Finally, he said, "Well that's great. I'm assuming it's something you are... good at, and like to do?"

After taking a slow sip of his Manhattan, Rob said, "I'm a videogame designer. Actually, a very successful one. Or was. I took a few years off."

Forest shook himself a little. Persian rug sales so completely defined Rob for him that he wasn't quite sure how to process this information. "So, you've been on a kind of sabbatical, then?"

"You could say that." Rob leaned against the bar next to Forest so that they were now facing the same way, which improved the dynamic immensely. "That job was anti-stress. It was something to do."

"I see." Clearly, a confession of some kind was percolating up out of this man. Forest just needed to wait. He took Rob's glass and began mixing them another drink.

"The thing was, I had an encounter," Rob said. "On the job at the design firm where I worked. Well, more than an encounter, really."

Here it was. Forest busied himself with putting the cherries away in the mini fridge.

Rob scratched an ear. "In fact, it was a rather long episode… of harassment."

"Really?" Why was Rob telling him this? He wondered if his role in this little dance was to probe for more information. "Co-worker?"

Rob accepted the fresh Manhattan. "No. Boss. Of the female persuasion."

"What? No. That doesn't happen, does it? Isn't it usually the other way around?"

"Usually. But it's more common than you think."
"Well, what kind of a…" Forest considered several possible ways to finish the sentence but stopped himself, certain he would say the wrong thing. And he was also positive that no answer Rob might provide would help him understand.

"She made me do things. To keep my job, to get bonuses, vacations. Of course I had two boys heading towards college. We needed the money, the bonuses. So…"

Forest forestalled the temptation to cover his ears and say "la la la" really loud until Rob stopped talking. He took a deep, steadying breath. "If you don't mind my asking, why did you allow this?"

Rob sighed and shook his head. "Classic."

"Beg pardon?"

"That's the classic question of people who have never suffered abuse."

"I mean," Forest floundered, "wasn't there some kind of a human resources department? Some higher-ups?"

"Nope. Too small an outfit. She was the CEO, so she was the *highest* up. And to answer your question about why, I think she saw me as… weak. Compliant. If you're a guy like me who has a family to feed, and especially if you have a kind of history of being under someone's rule…"

They were leaning against the bar side by side again. Forest looked at Rob. Dear God, he thought, was Pat some kind of man-eater? What the hell?

"Oh, not Pat," he said, answering Forest's unspoken question. "No, she's amazing. A good, strong, resilient, incredible woman. Honestly, she's the only reason I'm still here."

Forest didn't dare guess what that meant. He thought of the dinner conversation, and the hint at the kind of childhood Rob had. He also tried to remember anyone confiding in him like this before. It wasn't something that happened with any frequency. He rather prided himself in keeping people at arm's length. And this was precisely the reason. Why him? Why now?

As if reading his mind, Rob said, "Thanks for listening, man. Helps to get it off my chest. You get tired of keeping secrets." Then he suddenly pulled up a sleeve, revealing a line of hideous pockmarks dotting the inside of his arm.

Forest took a step back. "Shit! She did that to you?"

"Not my boss—my mother." Rob lowered his sleeve again. "She had a terrible habit with cigarettes." In the pause that followed, he looked up and seemed to be appraising Forest. "Why am I telling you all this? You're one of those who lives a blessed life. You've never had to experience abuse, I'm sure. But, well, I get a good feeling from you. Like you somehow get it."

Then out of nowhere, something swirled in Forest's memory. Dark robes and a back room. The thick smell of incense and a priest named Father Anthony. Hot breath, robes and skin. Innocence shattered. He shook his head in the practiced way that had been diffusing the memory's power since he was 11 years old. Then he turned to Rob, exhaling. But Rob was looking out the garden window into the night.

"Well, anyway," Rob said. "I had to do a lot of work… you know, on myself. And I'm ready to go back to what I was meant to do. Different company. Bigger. More buffer."

Forest nodded. "Congratulations."

"Yeah. Thanks. And so as it turns out, we won't be here long. And I'm sorry about all this. The disruption."

"It's okay," Forest said. He looked at Rob. "Really. I mean that."

Just then the women returned, rubbing their arms, and Pat admitted that she had gotten a little chilled out there.

Forest had the odd feeling that they had been gone a long time.

Rob put his arm around Pat's shoulder, and she leaned into him. He said, "Shall we turn in, sweetheart?"

"Will we be party poopers?"

Alexandra laughed. "You guys get some rest. I'm sure you're beat!"

When they had gone up the stairs, she poured herself another glass of wine and turned on the electric fireplace, then sat on the couch with a deep sigh.

Forest stood near the fire. "It was a nice evening. You put on a wonderful dinner."

She looked up at him, her eyes were bright from the wine. "Thank you. It's so nice, having people around."

"Well. I'm really sorry to tell you that it turns out they won't be here very long."

"Oh no. Forest, what did you say to Rob?"

"Nothing." He sat down with her on the couch, then awkwardly put his arm around her shoulder. He felt like a teenager. "He actually got another job, so he's ready to move on already."

She sighed and sipped her wine. "People are always moving on."

"Yes." He couldn't find the words he wanted, and the silence grew. But then Rexy jumped up to join them and spread himself across their laps and muttered soft, contented sounds.

Forest, knowing he must say something, but at a loss for how to say it, leaned down toward Rexy's ear and said quietly, "I've been thinking, old boy. What do you say we move back into town? Back where the people are, and the dog parks, and coffee houses and Mama's friends?"

He heard Alex make the slightest sound. It was almost nothing. A sigh or a slight intake of breath. But when he looked at her, he saw that tears were sparkling in her eyes, reflecting the light of the fire. And he thought perhaps if played his cards right she could forgive him, and they could start again.

11

Neighbors

Benny was at the window again, watching the new family across the street crawling around the property like wild animals. Not literally crawling. Just... everywhere.

He looked on, annoyed, as an indeterminate number of children occupied themselves with balls, bats, jump ropes, skateboards, trikes and bikes, and even small cars. One was Pepto Bismol pink and branded after the ever-popular Barbie, and a red one was painted in a fire engine theme. Horrible.

What appalled Benny most, however, was the evident head of the household. Almost as soon as the moving truck left, he had launched into multiple, unnecessary home improvement projects. He had ripped out shrubs and painted the bricks on the front of the house.

It had been a perfectly good house. Nothing wrong with it, whatsoever. Maynard had seen to that.

"Honey," Jane said. "Come away from that window. It's not a TV."

"It's much better."

Jane was putting out things for their morning coffee break. It was their habit ever since Benny retired. She put some cream puffs on a plate, and he fancied one even though his doctor told him to cool it on the sugar.

He liked coffee breaks with Jane. It was their time to talk, after their morning activities. Benny's morning was typically spent tinkering with projects in his workshop. Jane usually went walking with the other retired ladies in their neighborhood after breakfast. They would circle round and round the neighborhood, strutting in colorful sweatsuits like exotic birds.

One of the ladies had the whitest hair Benny had ever seen, and she wore turquoise or blue, creating a startling contrast like the whitewashed architecture of a Greek island. Another dyed her hair jet black and wore jewel-tones —ruby red or jade green. She introduced herself as Jasmine, but Benny suspected that her real name was

something like Eunice or Mabel and that she gussied herself up to meet men at the VA.

Now, Jane—she was different. Normal. She dressed
the part of a sensible woman in later midlife. Sure, she col-
ored her hair, but nothing alarming. Just a nice, under-
stated auburn. And she wore prudent jogging clothes in
pleasant, unalarming tones.

He picked up a cream puff. "How was your walk, my
dear?" Jane typically waited for Benny to start the conversation. She was somewhat deferential, even after forty-one
years of marriage, although in fact she was the strong one.
The bright one. It was Jane who did taxes, balanced ac-
counts, and handled hard news like a marine. He pre-
ferred not to think of their balance of power.

"It was wonderful. The birds were singing. And the
gardens are just exploding in color. The Hansons' cat had
kittens, and they were out playing on the lawn. They're
just so cute."

"Those people should have spayed the cat."

"Could we get one, Benny?"

"A cat?" Benny sat back. "Oh, I don't know, Jane. They
are a lot of responsibility. And they'll shred your curtains
without thinking anything of it."

"I don't care about the curtains."

"Well, I'm not excited about a cat." He set down his
cream puff. "It would probably outlive us." He was thinking of Maynard.

Jane blinked. "That's a terrible thing to say, Benny."

"Well. I just don't know." He looked out the window. The neighbor children were playing with their contraptions and making an unconscionable amount of noise. Two lanky boys played basketball in the driveway for hours. Each time they bounced the ball, the sound ricocheted off Benny's house.

There were some girls, too, all blonde and similar in height. He hadn't sorted them out at all. Plus, an assortment of younger children, moving around so quickly they couldn't be counted. And finally, there was a baby. It was usually dressed in boy colors and a baseball cap, and Benny had come to think of him as a boy. The girls carried him around and then let him toddle about. And then they would plop him in a playpen and ride bikes or draw pictures right on the driveway with chalk.

At this moment, one of the basketball-playing boys and one of the bike-riding girls had collided and there was a ruckus. Benny could hear it all. "Would you look at that, Jane? The little monsters."

"Shush, Benny. They're kids."

"I don't remember our kids doing that. They were well-behaved. And there were only two. Not a marauding mob. Anyway, where are the parents? Those kids seem to have very little supervision at all."

Jane cleared the plates, saying nothing more. He never knew what it meant when she did that, even after all these years, but he suspected it wasn't good.

The next day was Saturday. Benny liked to keep routines, in spite of being retired. Saturday was chore day. He noticed that the man from across the street was working in the yard.

Benny intended to do yard work as well but decided to wait until the neighbor was done.

He hated that awkwardness of being near people and not making eye contact. What were you supposed to do? Shout out "hello"? That seemed so intrusive. Better to just keep your head down and focus on your tasks.

Today he decided to wait out the neighbor and work in the house until the guy went inside. There was plenty to do. He took care of a squeaky door with some WD-40 and then peeked out the window. All was quiet. They must have gone off somewhere with the mother in their exhaust-spewing Suburban.

He watched as the man, whatever his name was—Rick or Dick, maybe—hauled out a ladder. It was not a pretty sight. The man was walking with it straight up, awkwardly trying to guide it to the intended destination. Benny shook his head. Everyone knows you don't carry a ladder that way. You're likely to crash into something.

He looked on as the man comically stumbled across the driveway, moving this way and that like a drunkard, while the ladder tilted and nearly fell. Then he kind of walked it like a stiff doll—left foot, right foot—to the house.

Maynard would have rolled over in his grave. In fact, Benny imagined just that—Maynard tossing and turning down there as this idiot with no common sense took over his house.

"Watching the neighbor channel?"

Benny turned to see Jane holding a basket of laundry. "Matter of fact, yes," he said. "Our neighbor just fell off the turnip truck. It's endlessly amusing."

Jane sighed. "Honey, there are better things to do. It can't be good for one's blood pressure to get all worked up about the neighbors."

"I'm not worked up. What makes you think I'm worked up?"

"You never lurked at the window watching Maynard working around the house."

"Maynard was an intelligent man, Jane. He knew what he was doing. He could build anything. Fix anything. Heck. Remember how he built that extension on the house? And the time he added the pergola with the retractable shade? This clown, by contrast, is likely to hurt himself by just putting up a ladder. That's my primary concern, here."

"Stop spying and take this basket of laundry downstairs to the washer for me, Mr. Man."

To keep the peace, he did as he was told.

Later, after a glass of milk and a cookie, he looked across the street. The house seemed quiet. He finally ventured out to give the lawn its weekly mowing. He pulled the lawn mower out of the shed, admiring the immaculate organization of his tools for a moment. Then he grabbed a rag and his fuel to prepare the machine.

"Hello there!"

Crap. Benny recognized the weird choirboy voice of Rick or Dick. He looked up.

"Hi neighbor," the man said. "Saw you out here and thought I would stop by. We met the day we moved in?"

"Yes, we did."

"Please tell your wife we really enjoyed the cookies. The kids gobbled them all up. I only got one." The man was holding a coffee cup, which he set on top of Benny's mailbox. Benny noticed that the man had two welts on his face and one on his neck.

He touched the one on his cheek. "Say. You don't know how to get rid of bees, do you? We have a hive in the tree right next to the house. I can hear them buzzing from the kitchen."

Benny shook his head. "Can't say as I've ever had that problem." The man must have climbed up on the ladder, with zero protection and no actual plan, to deal with the bees, and inevitably had gotten stung. He felt dismayed for missing it.

"I was hoping to take care of that while my wife and kids are off to the zoo for the day. I poked at it to see if I could knock it down, but that didn't exactly go well. Should I use some kind of spray?"

"Oh Lord no. They're pollinators. A nuisance, perhaps, but overall good, like butterflies and bats. They have a purpose." Benny hoped he wasn't glowering. Jane said he glowered at times. The thing was, Maynard would have known exactly what to do. He might have gone into the city office where they had all kinds of pamphlets about such things.

The neighbor looked back toward his house and the beehive. "Well, I'm going to have to figure something out. Of course, it's just one of the million things one has to do. Homeownership, eh?" He seemed eager to find some common ground.

Scratching at one of his welts, Rick or Dick said, "Well, thanks for your time, um, Ben, wasn't it?"

"Benny." No one ever called him Ben.

Just then a red Subaru pulled into the driveway. It was Benny's daughter Lacy, and her little girl, Rose. As Lacy stepped out from behind the wheel and reached into the back seat to unbuckle her daughter, the neighbor said, "Looks like you've got company, Benny. I'll be going."

"See ya," Benny said. It occurred to him that he had just missed the chance to get the man's name.

Rose came out of the car bouncing. She was wearing red-rubber ladybug boots with black polka dots and eyes on the toes. She bounced across the driveway. "Grampy!" She threw herself on Benny, where he was crouched near the lawn mower.

"Hello Sugar Plum," he said.

Lacy put out a hand as if she needed to avert disaster. "Whoa, Rosie. You must be careful with your elders. Hi, Dad."

He smiled. "Isn't this a nice surprise!"

Perhaps he was partial, but he thought Rose was an exceptional child. She already spoke in full sentences at the age of three. And she had the most startling, dark brown eyes and beautiful chocolate brown hair, thanks to the genetics of her father who was Guatemalan.

When Lacy had first started dating Fernando, Benny had cautioned her. "Are you sure? Wouldn't that add a layer of complication, being in a mixed-race marriage and all that?"

"Oh, for the love of God, Daddy," Lacy had said. "Could you at least pretend you're a little bit enlightened?" And that was the end of that. They were happy now. He could see that. And they had produced the most beautiful progeny he had ever seen. It also helped matters that Fernando could judge a good whiskey.

"Oh yes, chore day," Lacy said. "I could set my clock by your habits."

Benny silently agreed that habits and the clock were inextricably connected.

Rose, who was now leaning against Benny, said, "What'sat mean?"

Lacy laughed. "It means Grampy is just a teensy bit predictable. There's nothing terribly wrong with it. I mean unless you like change. And adventure. But anyway."

Lacy's brother Kevin had said the same thing before he left for a fishing trip in Alaska and never returned.

Benny turned to Rose. "What are the secrets of the day, my fair maiden?"

Rose closed one eye and looked at him sternly. "I can't tell you. Then they wouldn't be secrets."

"You certainly have a point."

Lacy peeled Rose off her grandfather, and they moved toward the house. "Let's go see what Grammy is up to, sweet pea."

That was when Benny saw Rick or Dick's coffee mug on his mailbox, right where he had left it. This was a new predicament. It was probably the neighborly thing to do to take it back to him. But he imagined getting drawn back into conversation about the bee situation.

He decided to leave the mug. If someone came by and stole it, or some teenage brat smashed it on the street, or what have you, it wouldn't be Benny's fault. He hadn't invited that fellow to come over to shoot the breeze. Anyway, if Rick or Dick was even one bit observant, he would notice he had left it behind. All he'd have to do was look out of his kitchen window, as any self-respecting home-owner would do from time to time, and he would see his prodigal coffee mug on the mailbox.

He finished tinkering with the lawn mower, started it up, and began his back-and-forth pattern across the lawn. Each time he went away from the mug he could think about other things, such as the upcoming bingo night at the VA. But each time he flipped directions and came back, there was the coffee mug, abandoned like a stray puppy. It was a rather nice mug in an unusual eggplant color. Which meant that if anything happened to it, there would probably be a partial set—perhaps seven mugs instead of eight. Benny couldn't bear it.

When he finished edging the lawn, he marched the mug over to the house across the street. He rang the door-bell but didn't hear a sound. It must have been broken. What was the neighbor going to do about that? He mentally apologized to Maynard and knocked hard on the door with his knuckles.

Rick or Dick opened the door, his face puffy and his hair a mess. He must have been sleeping. "Oh hey, Benny. Is that mine?" He took the mug with one hand and ran the other over his face. "That's super. Thank you, man. You're a champ. Seriously."

It seemed like a lot of fanfare for a mug, but Benny was exceptionally glad to be rid of it. He turned to go.

Rick or Dick called after him. "Your lawn looks nice, Benny! It looks great from here."

By now, Benny was walking back toward the house, so he just raised a hand in acknowledgment. He noticed that there were some dandelions just peeking up out of the neighbor's lawn, which was something Maynard would never have tolerated.

At home, Jane, Lacy, and Rose were working on a puzzle together. He kissed each of them on the head. "I think I'll work in the shop and let you ladies gossip."

Benny's workshop project was the repair of Maynard's old croquet set. He thought his grandchildren might like it someday. Maynard's kids had cleared out his house when he died. They had an estate sale, then a yard sale. Finally, they hauled the last of the stuff to Goodwill when there was almost nothing left but junk. Benny never went over there until the last day when he knew all the things that would actually remind him of Maynard were gone.

Bruce, Maynard's oldest son, and Laura, his only daughter, were there packing the last things into Bruce's truck for donation. Benny shook Bruce's hand and gave Laura a hug. Then he glanced around and saw the old croquet set. It was sitting in pieces on the lawn, and it looked destined for the trash can.

Laura sighed. "There's not much left, Benny. But if there's anything you want. Anything at all. You were pretty special to Dad."

Benny rocked back and forth on his heels. He hadn't wanted anything. He wanted Maynard not to be gone, was all. But he glanced over at the croquet set, which now sat alone at the edge of the lawn. "I might like that," he said, twitching his head in its direction.

Laura and Bruce looked at the set with him and for a moment no one said anything. Some of the mallet handles were broken. Everything was chipped and the paint was all rubbed off. Also, it appeared that a dog or perhaps a rat had chewed on some of the mallets.

"That," Bruce said, "is crap. You're not going to want that, Benny. How about his humidor? I don't know why this beauty didn't sell. Look at it." He held up the old humidor made from redwood burl that had held Cuban cigars. Benny remembered that it had sat on a side table near them on the nights they played cards, which was always out in Maynard's heated garage. This was out of deference to Carol, Maynard's wife, who had passed on some years before. Carol had never allowed any sort of smoking in the house. He thought of having a nice cigar with Maynard and the familiar aroma of the humidor.

"No thank you," he said to Bruce. "I'll take that croquet set. See if I can get it all fixed up. It will give me something to do."

Laura put all the pieces in an old floral gift bag, which was another of the last remaining items. Then she handed it to him and said goodbye in a small voice. And Bruce mumbled something too. Benny had watched those kids grow up in that house. Now he wasn't sure he would ever see them again. But he wasn't the type to make a scene. He thanked them and walked away.

Now he worked on the project in his workshop whenever he felt like spending a little time with Maynard. He would shoot the shit a little, and pretend Maynard was there to answer. Friendship didn't stop at death, in Benny's book.

"We're going to get this all fixed up good as new, Maynard."

"See, Benny? I told you that lathe would come in handy."

"You were right, my friend. As usual! This is why I reluctantly listen to you."

He laughed and imagined Maynard laughing too.

Maynard's funeral had been several weeks before the estate sale, on a Saturday in April, a dour time in Minnesota with dead grass and gray skies. On the day of the funeral, there was still gray slush on the roads from old snow. Leading up to that day, Benny had been thinking about how mad he was at Maynard for dying. Maynard hadn't taken good care of himself. "You old coot," he said as he dressed for the service. "I'm not going to say I told you so."

How many times had he said Maynard should get his blood pressure checked? How many times did he tell him to lay off the red meat and maybe eat a salad? But Maynard was persnickety. That was a fact.

For the funeral service, Maynard's family had asked Benny to say something, so he wrote some things down, and had to keep crossing off words like "stubborn" and swapping in "self-made man" and "heart of gold." He wasn't used to the idea that Maynard was gone, his house sitting empty after twenty-five years, and the end of all those times shooting the breeze as if they had forever ahead of them.

He edited the draft of his speech, and then he typed it up nice and made the font large so he wouldn't have to squint when he got up to speak.

When his time came in the program, he walked solemnly up to the pulpit. He had finally stopped feeling mad. Something else was going on entirely. He tried to brush it aside. He looked out at the people. His family sat together with Maynard's family. Jane sat next to Bruce and Laura, who were both crying. Jane held Laura's hand and he knew that would be comforting to her. She just had the right touch. Lacy and Fernando were there in the same pew, both looking nice. Lacy also had a tissue that she used to dab her eyes. And at that moment Benny realized Maynard had been like an uncle to her.

He adjusted his tie and looked down at the piece of paper in his hands, which swam with words. What had he written? What did it mean? "You old coot," he thought. But his mind said these words softly. Finally, when he opened his mouth to speak, no words came. The people waited and watched him, without a stir. As he wondered how long he had been standing there, the minister came to his rescue and offered to read what he had written to the congregation. Benny nodded and handed him the paper. And the minister read. He read the words perfectly, with just the right inflection here, and emphasis there. And it was beautiful.

When the minister was done, he handed back the paper to Benny and he smiled, and Benny thought that maybe it had all gone as well as it could have.

The croquet set was coming along, now. He was basically replacing everything, but that was okay. He liked how it gave him focus, now that the funeral was over, and Maynard's house had been cleaned out. Now that a new family had moved in. He turned on the lathe and began working the pattern into the wood. "I'm down to the last mallet handle, Maynard. Look at this. Is that a professional job, or what?"

"Bye Dad!" Lacy's voice called down the stairs to his workshop. "I need to get Rose home for her nap."

"Okay," he called up. "Thanks for coming by!" But he didn't go up. He was covered in sawdust and up to his gills in the project. He felt like Maynard was hanging out with him there, eyeing his work and maybe giving him a hard time. That's how he was.

A little later, as the paint dried on the mallet handles, he went to see what was happening upstairs. Jane was putting something on for dinner. He looked across the street to see that the mother and the kids had returned in the Suburban. They had groceries, and Benny tried to fathom how she went to the store with all those kids and managed to get anything done. Rick or Dick was out in the yard trying to use a trimmer, but he clearly didn't know what he was doing. He had a long cord and kept tripping on it. The kids were nearby, too, which was madness. You don't use trimmers and weed whackers around people without eye protection.

"Look at that, Jane. The guy is going to put someone's eye out with a flying pebble. Those things spit out rocks and pieces of earth." He turned away. "For once I can't watch."

"He watched you working in the yard today, you know."

"What? He did?"

Jane smiled. "Sure. This is probably the first home he has owned. He doesn't have the foggiest idea what to do. So, he looks to see what you do."

"What do I do, Jane? Nothing at all worth watching. That's what."

She shook her head. "Not true. You mowed the lawn, then you did all that edging. A little later, he made a trip to the hardware store to buy an edger."

"Oh no. Really? I am not taking responsibility for anything he may do. He's unqualified to be a home-owner!"

Jane quietly turned back to the stove. There it was again, that mysterious, silent behavior. He decided to try to soften a little. Perhaps he was, in fact, glowering.

After dinner, Jane went to the living room to watch an evening show and he returned to the window, which was open to let in the fresh evening air. The neighbor was done with trimming and evidently hadn't maimed anyone, and the kids were all playing in the yard and driveway. It would be so wonderful when the fall came, and most of them were back in school.

The parents had gone inside. The children were moving about on bikes and scooters. One boy practiced shooting baskets, then twirling the basketball on a finger. The baby was in the playpen playing with a toy or a book.

As he watched, the kids drifted into the house one by one. First, the basketball player walked into the garage, bouncing the ball off the bend in his arm and catching it. Then he shot it into a bin in the corner and walked into the house through the garage door. A few of the girls skipped their way into the garage and went in, with some younger ones running along behind. The other boy who was practicing jumping off a ramp with his skateboard deposited the board in the garage and went in as well. Finally, one girl in braids and a pink dress who had been reading a book in a folding chair got up and walked into the house with her nose still in the book.

They had left the baby outside.

Benny thought of going to get Jane. "Look at that, Jane," he'd say. "This is what I'm talking about. They have left the baby in the yard. They have too many kids to keep track of."

But he didn't do that. Someone should keep an eye on that baby. He thought of the things you read in the papers about abductions. Any second one of the baby's family members would realize that no one had the baby. Someone would come out and coo over that child and lift him out of the playpen and make sure he was okay.

No one came. The baby must have realized that he had been left alone because he pulled himself up and stood with his hands on the edge of the playpen and looked around. Then he began to call and make loud baby sounds. "Muh? Gah!"

"Scream," Benny said. "Go ahead. They might hear you if you scream."

"Mama?"

The thing that happened next made Benny's blood run cold. The beehive suddenly let loose from its hold on the tree and came crashing to earth, right near the playpen. When it hit the driveway, bees exploded out of it. The baby watched, fascinated, as they flew all around. But then he was stung. Even from here, Benny could see that multiple bees had landed on the baby's face and neck, and he was moving his arms now and crying.

Benny quickly took his cell phone from his pocket and dialed 9-1-1. "Ambulance," he said. "Baby. Multiple bee stings." He gave the address, yelled for Jane, and ran across the street, where he pounded on the front door of the house. The baby was wailing now, and Benny could hear a siren coming.

Jane walked across the street and joined Benny as Rick or Dick and his wife emerged from the house. They looked at each other as if to say, "I thought you had him!" Then the woman screamed. "Rodney!" She ran to the baby and lifted him out of the playpen as the ambulance pulled up and paramedics jumped out. The bees had settled and were now mostly interested in their fallen hive.

Rodney buried his face in his mother's shoulder as she spoke to the EMTs. Benny tried to count welts on the baby's head and neck, though the little tyke was crying and writhing. He counted six that he could see. Wasn't a lot of bee venom all at once dangerous, especially for a baby?

"Babies are rarely allergic to bees," one of the EMTs said over the wails of the boy. "But he has gotten a lot of stings. He needs to be seen. Let's get him to the medical center."

The parents looked at each other. Rick or Dick said, "I'll stay here with the other kids. You go."

Then the mom and the baby were loaded into the ambulance with one of the paramedics, and they sped away.

"Aww," one of the boys said. "He didn't even turn on the siren. What's the point of that?"

One of the girls was sniffling and whimpering. "Will he be okay?"

Rick or Dick let out a deep breath that he seemed to have been holding since he emerged from the house. "Yes. He will. Thanks to Benny, he's in good hands." He clapped Benny's shoulder. "You saved the day, my friend. I owe you a beer."

Benny felt unsteady. He looked at the bees. "It was nothing."

"No, man. I mean, you acted fast and did the right thing. You must have been looking out the window at just the right moment."

"Yes," Benny said. "It was quite a coincidence." He felt Jane's eyes on him. "We'll be going now." He took Jane's hand and they started to walk toward their house.

But then he turned back. "Oh, hey. What was your name again?"

"It's Rich. Short for Richard."

Benny nodded. He might have remembered that.

Later, over a glass of port, he and Jane talked about the day and how the garden was coming in, and about Lacy and Rose. Everything except what happened at the neighbors' house. "I'm almost done fixing up the croquet set," Benny said.

Jane squinted at him, as if she suspected him of something, like avoidance. "I'm sure Maynard would be pleased."

Benny didn't answer. He looked out the window and across the street to Maynard's place—only it wasn't Maynard's anymore. Things had gone quiet in the yard and lights had come on in the house. Night was falling, and an era was ending. Benny imagined giving Rich some pointers about home ownership. How to prune hedges, edge a lawn, carry a ladder. That sort of thing.

Magically, beyond the giant maple tree Maynard had planted so long ago, the moon rose golden and bright, illuminating the way forward.

Author's note: Neighbors was first published in August, 2023 in The Write Launch.

12

The River Bluffs

Gracie's brother stood at the very edge of the bluff, looking over. A breeze fluttered his t-shirt as he took a drink from an old army canteen. Crickets chirred like a far-off sawmill. Their song emanated from the dry grass, shrill and brittle like the sound of fear.

Griff pointed his canteen at the river. "Who do you suppose named it the Mississippi? The river source is here in Minnesota, and it runs through seven states. Makes no sense."

She shook her head and watched his outline silhouetted against the sky. She imagined his foot slipping, his arms wheeling as he fought gravity's deadly pull. This did not seem the time to be mulling about river names. "Griff, please get away from that drop-off. It gives me the heebie-jeebies."

He took another drink from the canteen, then tilted his head. "Gracie, how long have you known me?"

She blew out a puff of air that commingled with the warmth of the Minnesota sun. "I don't know. I'm sixteen, so I guess that long. You've been crazier than a bag of cats for two years longer than that. But I wasn't born yet."

"Damn straight. Sixteen years. I haven't fallen into a canyon yet, and I'm not about to now."

She pulled a bottle of water and a pair of binoculars from her backpack and sat down on a rock that seemed designed for the purpose—perfectly proportioned for a person's rear end to be cradled like a baby. She stared at Griff until he finally stepped away from the bluff's edge.

"I'm just not used to you," she said. "When we were kids and you went off with dad, I lost my sense of you. All your quirks."

He sat down on another rock placed nearby, as if someone had pitched the rocks there for conversations just like this. "Well, I sure as shit didn't forget you, little Sis."

"Hey!"

"What."

"I didn't say I forgot you, Griff. I never would. It's just. Well." She kicked at a stone with her boot, and it went tumbling off the edge, like a small death. She was thinking about the divorce, and the sudden and horrible moment when her father packed Griff into his car when she was nine years old, and they drove away. And how the periodic text messages and occasional visits could never fill the stone-cold cavern left by the messy, loud, hilarious kid he had been.

"I know," he said. "Our lives turned out different." He was looking out over the bluffs and valleys now, as if the lost years might be rolling by on a movie screen. "Hey look. Red tail."

She picked up the binoculars. The bird was magnificent, all form and intensity, with a tint of red at the back, glowing in the sun. It glided over the river bluffs, and Gracie imagined how that must feel. Soaring on air currents. Light and free.

"Cool," she said. "Let's hike."

They stood, put their packs back on and set out on the trail. There was the chuffing sound of boots on the dry path. The *screeee* of the red tail. Wind in the trees.

Unaccountably, it seemed melancholy. She and Griff should have had this all along — hiking and camping, popcorn on Saturday nights. Fights over the last piece of chicken. Not calendared appointments once or twice a year like trips to the dentist.

At least now they could both drive and they could sometimes make plans if they weren't too busy. But he was still so remote. A part of her that had been torn off. She could cling to this. Revel in the time with him. But then he'd be gone again. It made her hate him a little.

She wiped her brow with her bandana. The day had started cool, but now the heat emanated from the dusty trail and the rocks and pines. June bugs sang in the trees, and it seemed to be the song of heat.

"I have a friend who's bulimic," she said into the silence.

They were walking single file, with Griff in the lead. He glanced at her over his shoulder. "Crap. I've heard of that. It's kind of like an addiction, I guess."

They kept on walking for a while. Then Griff said, "Did she tell you? I mean, how did you find out?"

"Sometimes I just know things, you know? I figured it out. My friend leaves for the bathroom right after lunch every day. And she gets weird if anyone asks to go with her. It's just… I don't know. Bizarre behavior."

"That doesn't mean she's bulimic. It's not like that's the only explanation."

"No, I'm sure of it," she said. There were other details. She'd heard the noise of it. The double flushing. And there was a smell in the bathroom. She wasn't about to say any of these things out loud.

Griff raised his shoulders in a shrug. "I'm just saying. I mean, maybe the girl likes a few minutes alone in the bathroom after lunch. No crime in that."

"Griff, you're not even hearing what I'm saying. I *know*. That's all."

"Sure. Okay. What do I know? But I mean… well, what are you going to do?"

She snorted. "What *can* I do? Can you imagine? Someone you know has got this deep dark secret, like they just love to watch porn with their cat, or they are addicted to eating sofa cushions like those people on reality TV. But they totally don't want a single person to know about it. And you're supposed to call them out? Like, 'Hey, I notice you've got this weird problem, and you're trying to hide it. But you're not fooling anyone, pal.'"

Griff didn't answer. Minutes passed. That was just fine. She didn't want him to talk. This was exactly the whole entire problem with being a teenager from a messed-up family. No one gets you at *all*. And there's no one to talk to or give you any advice. She thought of her mother's boyfriend, Charlie, and how he tried to make sure she felt included. How he'd even give her a nudge and say, "Hey kiddo. Tell me what's going on in that complicated noggin of yours." Didn't he understand that trusting people was the hardest thing in the world?

They arrived at an overlook, with the bluffs all around and the silvery Mississippi snaking along way down below.

"So…" Griff said after a while. "I've never had a friend with that problem specifically. But believe it or not I've had friends with other problems. And you don't have to call them out. I'm not even suggesting that. Maybe you could literally just ask her if she's okay. Let her know she has someone to talk to."

Gracie nodded, though he wasn't looking. The truth was, she felt sad for Hannah, the girl with bulimia. She was probably stuck inside the lie she was living. Trying to keep up appearances. Not letting anyone in and feeling awful and alone.

She closed her eyes and breathed in the aroma of the pines and wondered what Griff's friends were like. He had a whole life away from her. What did they do? He was going into his senior year at a high school on the far east side of the Twin Cities, and she lived way down in southern Minnesota, in the town of Whimden. Sometimes her high school teams played his school if they went to state. She had once gone to a state baseball game with her friends and pointed out Griff playing first base. "That's my brother," she said. And they acted like she told them her father was Santa Claus, which of course no one would believe. "What? You have a brother? Oh my God, Gracie. Such a liar!"

They were walking again. Griff was whistling something. He was pretty good. She didn't know he could do that.

"Remember that family camping trip?" she asked. "A little while before the divorce when we went to the north woods?"

"We did?"

"Yes. It was up by the Mississippi headwaters. No one could forget that. We packed into the camping area with canoes. And we brought all this food and then dad figured out how to hoist it up into a tree at night away from the bears. But they got some of it anyway."

"Bears?"

"How could you forget that, Griff? We heard them in the night, and I was so terrified and dad kind of growled at me to keep quiet and then I was even more scared."

"Damn. It's seriously not coming back to me."

The buzz of the insects now seemed like the soundtrack of her mood. "Griff, that doesn't make any sense. The whole reason we went was because of you. You threw this fit that we hadn't gone camping or done anything fun outdoors in, like, forever. And our parents, who had it out for each other like a couple of rabid wolverines packed us all up. It was literally the very last thing we did as a family."

The red-tailed hawk made its forlorn cry. Maybe it was the same one. Maybe a different one. She imagined that sound meant the hawk was sad for her and her only-child life.

"You're not making that up, Gracie? No, never mind. I've forgotten all about that, is all. Come on."

He turned around at a bend in the path and started back down the way they had come. She followed along behind. But he seemed far away from her, just like when they were miles apart, each with their designated parent.

She thought of her father—a twitchy, easily irritated man, whom she barely knew now. She could not remember what he was like as the head of the household, or in day-to-day life. But the way he handled things like a spill on the carpet or car keys gone missing, vocalized in shrill accusations of anyone nearby, were burned into her mind.

"Water break," Griff said, as they came again to the scenic overlook. Two pregnant women were there, having a heated conversation about circumcision.

"I'm not cutting my son's foreskin off," said the one in purple, who was fanning her pretty, puffy face with her hand. "Why can't people mind their own business?"

The other one was dressed in a huge floral jumper that visibly amplified her size, and Gracie immediately felt sorry for her. A pregnant person evidently had limited choices in flattering clothing. The floral woman shook her head. "It's like the natural community constantly has to defend its views. Even from our own families."

They were in their own mini universe and didn't seem to notice Griff and Gracie.

"I'm going right home and giving my mom a piece of my mind," said the one in purple that Gracie had come to think of as Grape.

"As you should," said the one she thought of as Flowerpot.

Griff and Gracie exchanged a look. She tried to think of something else to occupy her mind, to erase the lingering question of whether that procedure had been done to Griff as a baby. Perhaps the answer would tell her something about the parents she had, and who they were as a family back then. "Are you...?"

"Yes I am," he said. And he looked away over the bluffs to the river.

This notion settled against a backdrop of all she didn't know about him, and a realization that wishing for the family she had lost was completely pointless.

When they returned to the last bluff, where their hike had begun, they both stood at the edge looking down to the river. Her head felt mossy from the heat and the dizzying view at the drop-off.

They would be leaving. Separating again. It was the same, sad, predictable result every time. And one day, it would just be over because he'd be busy with a wife and kids, or he'd move to another state.

Her breath caught in her chest for a moment, as pain and clarity came together, like a divining rod finding gold. She had a sudden breathtaking thought. A complete idea so real that she could picture it. As if watching a little movie reel of the immediate future, she imagined them grabbing hands right then, and taking a running leap into thin air, right at this spot, in a terrifying yet perfectly legitimate death pact. The gesture would send a message to their parents. "See what you did? You caused this. But you will never tear us apart again."

Her hands shook as this idea came to life as a foregone conclusion. The natural order. The only choice.

"Griff…."

But he cuffed her on the arm just then, and said, "Come on, Sis. Let's scram. Buy you a Coke on the way home." And then the urge melted away like a mirage.

"Guess what," he said in the car.

"What?"

"I'm applying to the local college—to Whimden. They have a great baseball team. My coach says I can make it. Then I'd be right here in town. I'd be able to see you more often. You could come to my games."

Tears began to sear her eyes and she blinked. "Really? That would be cool." She looked out the window at the passing trees and houses and willed the tears away by thinking of other things. "Guess what."

"What?"

"Mom's getting married to Charlie."

"No shit!"

"Yeah, they have been dating for like a year. Seems pretty legit. You'd like him. He's funny."

She glanced at his face and saw that he was smiling.

"Imagine that," he said. "Good for Mom."

She thought of Griff being right nearby at Whimden College, and a vision came to her of him coming to dinner—the four of them having a barbecue together on her mom's patio. Swimming in the pool. Acting like a family. A new one, whole in its own way. And with the car's stereo on, and the road disappearing beneath the wheels, tomorrow again seemed possible and almost real, like a materializing apparition.

Coming soon from the author

Somewhere in Minnesota captures life-changing moments from the perspective of several different characters. You may have noticed in the final story, *The River Bluffs*, that the main character is from a town called Whimden, Minnesota. Whimden is a fictional college town located in Southern Minnesota along the banks of the Mississippi river. The short stories in Jayna Locke's next collection, The *Whimden Chronicles*, all take place in this odd, bustling—and sometimes creepy—little college town. From murder mysteries to ghost stories, the tales in this collection uncover what really goes on in Whimden.

Get notified when the next book is released

To hear about the release of *The Whimden Chronicles*, find the sign-up form here: bit.ly/ContactJayna.

Or follow Jayna on Amazon at:
https://www.amazon.com/author/jaynalocke.

Information for book clubs, bookstores and more

If your book club, bookstore, writing group or other organization would like to invite Jayna to a reading or Zoom discussion, get in touch via this contact page: bit.ly/ContactJayna.

You can also reach Jayna through her website, www.jaynalocke.com, or on X (formerly Twitter) at www.twitter.com/@jaynatweets.

Book club discussion questions

Somewhere in Minnesota

1. Questions for *Last Night in Fargo*:
   - Teri is struggling with her feelings for Carl after having had a romantic encounter on her business trip. What are some of the factors that can drive a wedge in a relationship?
   - Do you think Teri just had a weak moment on her business trip, or are the challenges and differences in her relationship with Carl possibly insurmountable?

2. Questions for *Prodigal Father*:
   - The author chooses to write from the perspective of a 12-year-old boy. Is it believable?

- Max finds three perfect blue robin's eggs abandoned in a nest. What do they symbolize in the story?

- Max's father sometimes seems to tower over him, and other times seems old and shrunken. Why do you think Max sees him in both ways? And does one of these views of his father seem most true? Further, are we all multiple versions of ourselves, sometime great and sometimes small?

3. Questions for *Ripples*:

   - The primary conflict in this story is that Jeffy has run out onto a lake covered with melting, unstable ice. What are the other conflicts?

   - If Madeline hadn't figured out how to get onto the lake with the canoe to save Jeffy, what do you think would have happened?

   - How are egos and storytelling explored in the story?

4. Questions for *The Picnic*:

   - Josh experiences a range of feelings and emotions, yet outwardly he is rather unemotional and stolid. Does this serve him well, or does it cause some of the problems that occur in the story? What causes people to "keep their cards close to their chest"?

- If you could give Josh one piece of advice, at what point in the story would you do so, and what would it be?

- Marriage and commitment are key themes in this story. What are the different ways these themes play out? How does this tie into the concurrent theme that none of us truly knows what the future holds?

5. Questions for *The Walled City*:
   - Why do you think the city of Lucca, Italy was chosen as the setting for a story timed with the beginning of the Covid 19 pandemic? What is the significance of a city surrounded by enormous fortress walls?

   - Discuss how beginnings and endings are featured in this story. Vulnerability and innocence are also themes that could be interesting to discuss.

   - What do you remember about the initial days of Covid 19, before it was declared a pandemic? While this historic event was a clear demarcation in modern history and happened at the very beginning of the 2020 decade, to many people the timeline of what happened and when is a blur. Why do you suppose that is the case?

6. Questions for *Cast Off*:
   - This story ventures into magical realism, a genre in which a story is told very realistically, yet things happen which do not occur in real life. Did you get the sense that the alternate reality things Jules experiences are real in the context of the story? Or are they things she imagines?
   - The name of the story has multiple meanings. What are they and which did you think of as you read the story? Are they symbolic in some way?

7. Questions for *Hiding in Plain Sight*:
   - Delia ends up in a homeless encampment, on the run from her abusive husband. Why does she choose this instead of going to her mother or her best friend, or to a women's shelter?
   - The minister in this story reads a psalm about despair and then provides his take on it. He says it is always darkest before the dawn, and that in those moments "We discover that the grit and determination we have needed all along reside deep within, and that the moment

has come to lift ourselves up." Some are skeptical as he gives this sermon. Discuss whether you would find this message uplifting if you found yourself unexpectedly homeless.

- Michael is a former drug addict and homeless person and is therefore perhaps not a good candidate as Delia's knight in shining armor. But is there cause for hope that there is a good reason for these two people to have accidentally crossed paths again under these peculiar circumstances? Why are some people "good on paper" but, in reality, are insufferable humans, while others have seemingly terrible curriculum vitae and yet have a richer inner life and more to give?

8. Questions for *The Usher*:
- Frederick is tied in knots by finding a $100 dollar bill that does not belong to him. While it's not a lot of money, for someone of very limited means like Frederick, it's enough to cause serious angst. What would you have done in his shoes? Do you think any given person in his situation might feel differently depending on their circumstances and station in life?
- Frederick underestimates several things in this story. He underestimates the effect it will have

on him to hold onto the hundred dollars. He also underestimates Jimmy, and it therefore comes as a huge surprise that Jimmy is not only taking classes but pursuing a degree that will elevate him out of the minimum wage job. And finally, he underestimates himself. Discuss Frederick's transition over the course of the story. What do you think will happen next for him?

9. Questions for *Three Things*:
   - This story attempts to capture the difficult challenge of helping someone who is experiencing deep depression. The reaction of the neighbor, Victor Fisher, to Ollie's depression is juxtaposed against Linda's. Where Victor has no tolerance, Linda tries to understand and be supportive. Do you think she succeeds?
   - Discuss different societal approaches to mental health issues. For example, Linda attempts to identify the cause of Ollie's depression, as if she can reverse engineer it. And there are several analogies used in the story to compare depression to things that can be fixed by a surgeon or a mechanic. Why is it so difficult for people to deal with a person who is struggling with

mental health problems? As a society, have we become better at this over time?

10. Questions for *The Lake Home*:
   - This story is told from the perspective of Forest, who is rather arrogant. Discuss whether he is a likable character, and how his character changes as the story progresses.
   - Of all the things that happen on the night when Alexandra's family comes to stay, what do you think is the catalyst for Forest wanting to move back to town and make his wife happy?
   - What role does pride play in this story?

11. Questions for *Neighbors*:
   - Why does Benny get so worked up about what his new neighbors are up to?
   - It becomes apparent that Benny is somewhat emotionally stunted. How is this manifested throughout the story, and what changes for him by the end?
   - Benny clearly misses his old neighbor, Maynard. Discuss Benny's approach to managing his grief, and what aspects of that serve him well, and which don't?

12. Questions for *The River Bluffs*:

- Gracie misses Griff even when she is with him. Why do you think that's the case?
- This story discusses the notion of family, and the trauma of a family breaking apart. While no two families are the same, do you think it is part of the human condition that many people wish for some notion of a traditional family?
- The story climax has Gracie thinking about leaping off the edge of the bluff with her brother. Discuss what drove her to such an extreme, and how she recovered from that terrible momentary desire.

www.ingramcontent.com/pod-product-compliance
Lightning Source LLC
Chambersburg PA
CBHW060404310726
48976CB00003B/935